A SMALL LIGHT IN THE DARKNESS

Christiane Knight

Three Ravens Press

OTHER BOOKS BY CHRISTIANE KNIGHT

In Sleep You Know
Cast a Shadow of Doubt
BOOKS 1 & 2 IN STORIES OF THE ELERIANNAN

A Third Kind of Madness
A STORY OF THE ELERIANNAN

LEARN MORE AT CHRISTIANEKNIGHT.COM

A SMALL LIGHT IN THE DARKNESS

CHRISTIANE KNIGHT

Published by Three Ravens Press
PO Box 502 , White Marsh MD, 21162 USA
CHRISTIANEKNIGHT.COM

Cover design, book interior, and formatting: C. Knight
Cover image original photo: Larm Rmah from Unsplash
Interior Page Divider by Alderdoodle, https://ko-fi.com/alderdoodle
Silhouette of a Flock of Birds: GDJ from Pixabay
Brain Illustration: StarGladeVintage from Pixabay
Trees in Forest Silhouette: Hikmat Studios

ISBN: 978-1-73685-034-3 (print)
ISBN: 978-1-73685-035-0 (epub)
Library of Congress Control Number: 2026905863
First Edition, April 2026.

For Rose, who was supposed to stick around longer. I miss you.

CONTENTS

CHAPTER ONE

I'm lost in the echoing city streets, but the woods still call my name. Looking for someone who remembers glassphalt and thought it enchanting, which is why we don't have it anymore, right? Noth ing magical stays around here for long but us, wan dering and wondering why we're so alone.

Extra points for listening to music when you should be sleeping, staring out windows hoping for a glimpse of something unexpected, or being the one that people bring the pretty rocks and feathers to show.

I looked at the words I'd typed into the text box, as florid and cryptic and utterly desperate as anything I had published in my youth in shitty little copier-paper 'zines, the kind you can only buy in alternative bookstores and tiny record shops, harder to find every day. I had a handful of pen pals from those frail publications, and we all sent each other the same kind of words interspersed with heavily edited details about our lives. It was enough to feel a genuine connection, but all of us suffered the same issue: we were incredibly lonely and had failed to find someone like us nearby. We were limited to words in emails, letters, and social media posts.

It's not that we couldn't video chat or call each other. We could, and did once or twice, but it never felt right. The magic wasn't there; it made me anxious, and I tried too hard. I always imagined that the other person was left disappointed by who I actually am. Not pretty enough, with a goofy accent, not poetical or clever, just a weirdo who seemed much cooler on paper.

I needed a title for the post. The stupid AI assistant that continually attempted to insert itself into even the most mundane tasks suggested "anachronism lovers" for an opener. I hated that immediately. It was clunky, unpoetic, and most importantly, not at all what I was trying to convey. I didn't eschew the aesthetic of present times. I just wanted to enhance it with things that seemed to matter less than they used to. There was a part of me that wondered what might happen in the future if they finally did figure out how to make AI live up to what they promised it would be. Would it ever be convincing enough to fool me, or understand what I wanted?

I decided on "gathering up the stars, hand in hand" because it evoked what I was yearning for, and double-checked that I used my throwaway email account. After I'd made sure that I specified "Baltimore" and agreed to the posting rules, I held my breath and hit "Publish."

It wasn't the first time I'd done this, throwing the equivalent of a letter in a bottle into the electronic ocean while hoping for the best. Usually, I'd get a smattering of replies, most of which were thinly veiled attempts to get into my pants despite the email-writer having no idea what I looked like. If all I were interested in was getting laid, I'd be set. Of course, that also might come with a side of getting murdered, but so does regular dating. One thing I'd come to realise is that the people who use these sections of the bulletin board—including me—like to take risks. I got these responses because eventually, the people trolling the boards find what they're looking for.

Occasionally, I'd get something a little more meaningful. There was a guy who traded messages with me for a while who was really into riding bikes and squatting in city-owned properties, and he always had interesting stories to tell. He explained to me about how he and his friends would create comfy spaces in the woods near the Jones Falls, complete with furniture to make it feel like a living room surrounded by trees. I always marveled that they never got caught in their urban camping adventures, but one thing I've noticed about Baltimore is that if you act like what you're doing is normal, especially if you're a white dude, most people won't question you, not even cops. As soon as they get a whiff of guilt, though, all bets are off.

There were a few other poetry writers or lyrics quoters that posted regularly, but I never connected with any of them, not for lack of trying. The impression I got is that they wanted to be the star of their show, the one that someone else thirsted for. There's no room for two of the same types in their world, or at least that's how it felt. Which...fair enough. Far be it from me to judge why someone would be looking for anonymous validation from the Internet. I mean, it would be disingenuous for me to look down at anyone else's motivation when I'm doing something similar.

It took a week to get a response that wasn't nonsense.

Sandwiched between emails with titles like "I know what you really need" and "Let's meet up and play!" was a response that just had "Fomalhaut" in the subject line.

I didn't recognize the word at first, so I looked it up online and read everything I could find on the subject. Known as the Loneliest Star, it was the kind of reference I immediately related to, and obscure enough that it felt clever. Now to see if the attached message lived up to that opening.

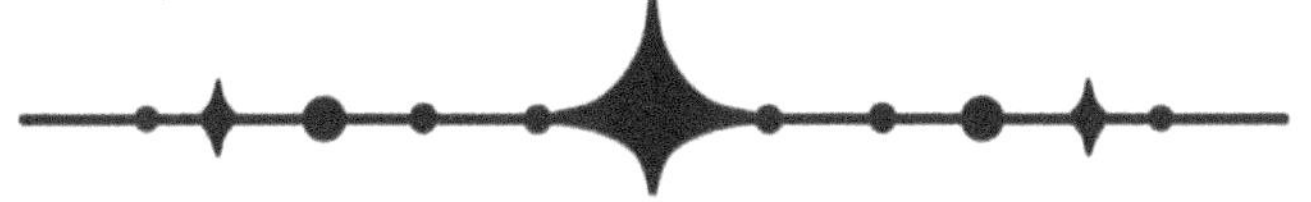

`I am new to everything despite having been here for years, so the simplest things are all treasures to me. No one seems to find the joy in the everyday that I do. They don't see the beauty because to them it's so common as to be unremarkable.`

`A light that's not reflected back surely must dim over time—or is that just hope diminishing, thanks to loneliness? Imagine how solitary those far flung stars must feel, yet they keep shining on, faithfully. I wish that I had their fortitude.`

`Who are you?`

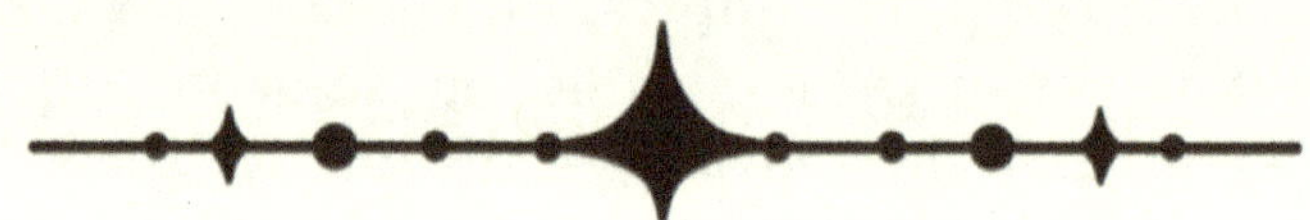

Wow. I didn't know who this person was, but I needed more.

They asked who I am, and I wasn't sure how to answer that. How much should I reveal at the outset, while keeping this intrigue going? Suddenly, I felt pressured. I'd never had a response this perfect before, and I didn't want to blow it.

I thought about it for a while before I started typing. I knew I could maintain a facade of mystique and wonder. It would be easy enough; I'd been writing like this my whole life, well before I started sending these sad yet hopeful little missives out into the ether.

But this time, I wanted to be the person I honestly am: both poetic and dreamy, and also someone who goes to work at a dreadfully mundane job and drops crumbs down her cleavage and wishes that people would take a moment to look around them. I couldn't have an authentic connection if I only showed an idealized version of myself, could I?

And that's what I thirsted for, that true connection. I spent my days with my body going through the paces of living a normal life, more or less, while my mind went on non-stop with an internal monologue about all the things I saw and the potential that other people seem to ignore. I've been told I'm the walking personification of "stop and smell the roses", and that's not wrong. I know there are others out there like me, but the struggle to find them left me feeling more isolated every day.

I'm a human in conflict, because what passes for life these days doesn't seem to have room for what I treasure. Yesterday, I noticed a small pink flower growing from a crack in the curb, close to where cars whizzed by, ignored by people rushing to jobs where they'll sit at a desk and look at mind dulling papers or screens for the rest of the day. I feel a deep kinship with that blossom, persevering in a hostile environment and even managing to bloom.

I'm moved by art and music, but even more by blue skies and trees that spread their canopies confidently across that sky. I'm often melancholy, but I'm also joyful. Are you also full of conundrums?

You can call me Tryst, if you like.

Maybe it was too soon to give anything to identify me—Trystin is my given name—but I was feeling bold and maybe a little reckless, bolstered by the quality of their response. I knew that giving a little sometimes gets you more, and teasing out the personal bits in these exchanges is half the fun. I felt a little flutter when I hit send. I was already enjoying this.

I didn't hear anything back for two days.

I went through my routine as usual, while I tried not to check my inbox too many times. My boss, Janine, would catch me glancing at my device for the thousandth time and gently make fun of me for caring so much about messages from strangers. I probably shouldn't have told her about my wannabe pen pal situation, but we're friends, and besides, I thought that someone should probably know in case I unexpectedly disappeared or something.

I worked at a little artsy boutique in Remington called Under The Leaves. We kept ourselves afloat by handling art purchases and decor for local hotels and businesses with public-facing spaces that wanted to convey a certain aesthetic. There was often a lot of downtime between clients. Janine usually gave me that time to focus on my own projects, but it also allowed my mind to worry about things over which I have no control. Like, of course, the gap between replies from someone interesting.

They're a normal person, with a job and a life, I told myself. They're busy. It's only been two days. What do you expect? They're probably not even as interested in all of this as you are, because you're the only loser with nothing else to keep you going here.

I gave myself this lecture at least five times in those two days. It didn't really stick.

And then on the third day, I found a reply.

You are a determined flower, and I'm a lonely star. One reaches for the light, and the other may be too far away to provide what's needed, though it shines brightly. Still, I'll try.

What makes you melancholy, Tryst? What brings you joy?

I spend my time researching, learning about humanity and the world around us. I find it delight ful and horrific in turn, and yet I'm always left wanting to know more. For all my studies, I haven't been able to connect with people in meaningful or immersive ways—not until now, I should say. That is, if you decide to continue this conversation!

link to video clip of Fatalism by Massive Attack, Ryuichi Sakamoto & Yukihiro Takahashi Remix

Watch this tonight, in the darkness before sleep, and I believe you'll know me a bit better.

Know them a bit better? I didn't even know what to call them.

In my mind, they became Fomalhaut because to name something is to claim a kind of ownership over it, and the title of the star they referenced in their first email was the only name I had. Not that I wanted to own them. But there was a part of me that already whispered, "This could be mine", despite knowing so little about what it was grasping.

That "still I'll try" really won me over.

I wrote the following response quickly, dismissing the intrusive AI assistant after it gave me one too many irrelevant suggestions.

Like you, the world brings me much joy and is also a source of my melancholy. Watching people be cruel to each other just because of where they were born, or who they love, or even things too small to matter—that makes my heart hurt. But I find some melancholy things beautiful, if painfully so. The ache from a piece of moving music, or watching a tragic movie, when you know that the characters aren't real but their suffering evokes a sadness born of empathy. Those things appeal to me.

Joy comes from so many sources! Often they're simple ones: an unexpected meeting of friends, with tight hugs, or spotting a murmuration of starlings as they swirl over the rooftops at sunset.

I expected a similar share in return, but what they wrote next was surprising.

I have never seen a murmuration nor heard of it

until you mentioned it.

I had to do a search for the phenomenon. You've seen these happen in person? The birds move in great clouds and don't collide, even without a leader or a chosen path. Coordination without communication, only observation.

Humans could learn much from these birds.

link to video clip of two women in a small boat, delighted as a murmuration appears over them and puts on a show of swooping and diving

This exchange began an intense back-and-forth between us over the next couple of days. We talked about stars and space exploration, and the hubris of humans to want to wander into inhospitable surroundings when we couldn't be bothered to fix the messes we'd made here on the home planet. I quoted my favorite poem by Keats, "To Autumn", and explained in detail why the phrase "touch the stubble-plains with rosy hue" felt so vibrant and evocative to me. They would send me links to interesting things they found in their daily research, as widely varied as a video on why wombat poop is square, a virtual tour of the National Gallery of Art, or a long essay about the creeping fascism that was once again happening around the world. I mentioned the idea of figuring out how to take the virtual tour together, and there was a noticeable break in replies for a couple of hours before I received a cautious affirmative.

Later that day, they suggested that we could text in addition to emailing each other.

I have written a program, a virtual world ap plication that is small and easy to use for private communication. It works on handheld devices and com puters. It's encrypted, and we can send anything we like back and forth. I promise there are no viruses or exploits to fear. Would you consider it?

link to download Sui Generis app

This time, I was hesitant, which didn't make any sense. Wasn't I the one who suggested doing a virtual tour together? I upped the ante, and now they were calling my bluff. Nothing here could be linked directly to me, and if I ever wanted to end things, both my anonymity and theirs would be safe—at least in theory. It had me nervous, but wasn't that why I'd started this conversation in the first place, to meet people like me?

I waited until I was home before I downloaded the app to my devices. I ate dinner, took a shower, and talked to my housemates about all the normal things—but I couldn't stop thinking about talking to my mysterious acquaintance, and I knew I was going to try out this program even if I felt unsure about changing how we communicated.

I finally announced that I was going to bed and said goodnight. Once I was in the comfort of my bed, my room illuminated only by the device's screen, I opened the link in their last message and started the download. The best part? The pop-up message that asserted it would turn off the AI assistant because of program conflicts, and to close the program now if this was an issue. That was a bonus, as far as I was concerned.

They were right, it seemed easy to use. I clicked on the icon, and it opened into a no-nonsense screen: a black background with white text in an old-school terminal font, complete with the blinking block cursor after the request "NAME?"

Wow, throwback. It felt funny using the device's keyboard to type, but I answered "Tryst" and was rewarded with a graphic of the screen filling up with overlapping text that faded away to reveal a customization screen. I could choose plain text or graphics, so I went for the latter.

"ENTER ANY WORD OR PHRASE FOR YOUR AVATAR."

Any word or phrase? A million possibilities passed before

my eyes before I decided to see what would happen if I chose "murmuration." The screen blurred for a moment, and then I was presented with a surprisingly lifelike animation of a flock of starlings, swooping and diving in synchronization.

"OK?"

I pressed the button, and the scene changed into a realistic-looking landscape of an open field, with trees in the distance and a blue sky above. I found controls in the settings at the bottom left that turned on and off the nature sounds, and when I touched the bottom middle, a text box with a blinking cursor popped up.

I didn't know how to find Fomalhaut to talk to them. They said it was private, but surely it couldn't just be the two of us there? The app was certainly well-made, nicer than some of the paid ones on my device. I decided the easiest way to go was to announce myself, so I tapped open the text box.

`Hello?`

I realized that after I hit enter, the murmuration started to move, a cloud of birds slowly sweeping from one side of the screen to the other in a flowing mass. It was a lovely effect, and again I wondered how it was achieved with such a small program. I'm no expert, but I've been online for a long time and I've used many different programs to connect with other strangers to share interests and connect on various levels of meaningfulness. And this one was unlike anything I'd seen. It felt more like a high-powered game, both visually and in how smoothly it ran. The graphics looked like I was watching a movie in super high resolution.

My assessment was interrupted when a brightly lit orb appeared in the middle of the meadow.

It was almost too brilliant to look at directly at first, but the light dimmed gradually to a more comfortable level. I had no idea what was going on until text appeared at the bottom of the screen.

I'm here. I'm glad you decided to try this method.

A pause, then the words on the screen were replaced.

There are also voice capabilities available. Talk to text, or we can choose to speak to each other directly. All your choice, of course.

I considered that possibility. Was I ready for this person to hear my voice? And what did they sound like—deep voiced, high-pitched, softly spoken, someone who talked a mile a minute?

I decided to be honest.

I feel I'm much more interesting and together in text. Maybe that's just me being nervous, but when I type out responses, I have time to consider my statements and know they're coherent. Would you be disappointed if I waited a little until I felt more comfortable?

The orb pulsed for a moment, a subtle shift in brightness.

I want you to always feel comfortable around me. You should use whatever method of communication feels safest and natural for you.

There was a pause. More pulsing. It was almost hypnotizing to watch.

If this container is too strange, we could go back to the other…

It's difficult to pick up emotion from text, but that was a sad-sounding statement if I'd ever heard one.

No, this is beautiful! You did all of this yourself? Am I the first person to use it besides you? I've never seen anything like it.

...you know, if *you* would rather talk instead of type, that would be okay. As long as you don't mind me typing in answer?

Pulse, pulse, pulse.

I waited, watching the starlings circle about in one section of the sky. I noticed they became more active when I typed. If I put my finger on the screen, I could drag it and change perspective, moving across the field closer to the trees, or tilting up to look at the sky.

I almost jumped out of my skin when the voice boomed out of the tiny speaker.

"Will this—is this okay?"

I scrambled to turn down the volume to a reasonable level and muttered, "Once you're not yelling at me, sure. Okay, maybe say something again so I know how loud it'll be?"

Then I laughed at myself, because, of course, I hadn't enabled voice, so they couldn't hear me. He? It was a masculine voice, though I knew that didn't mean anything. I figured I'd better ask.

Can you say something else? Just so I can check the sound. I had it cranked up while I was listening to music earlier, and I forgot to turn it down. And... what should I call you? What pronouns do you use? I should have asked this long ago; I'm sorry.

Why was my face so hot?

"Is this better?" The voice was masculine, but there was something slightly off about it, and I couldn't figure out what it was. "Pronouns don't matter much to me, truthfully. What name have you used so far? What do you call me in your head?"

Um. I don't exactly call you anything, but in my head, I associated you with Fomalhaut, because, well, you know.

"Because I referenced the Loneliest Star."

Yes. I didn't have any other kind of reference, like what you look like or, well, anything. And that's okay! I want to know you for who you are on the inside.

"But you gave me a name, and I didn't return the trust. I am sorry. Fomalhaut is as good as any, but you can call me whatever you like, and you can use "he" or "they". That would be... okay."

The way they said "okay" was odd, uncomfortable. And considering their usual tone in the messages we exchanged, it could well be more casual than they were used to. Which might mean that they were nervous too, but trying to loosen up with me. For me? Or maybe I was reading too much into things. There was still something not quite right, and I couldn't figure out what that was.

I decided to let it go for now. It was just another mystery that I might get an answer to later, if I was lucky.

CHAPTER TWO

My days started to become a race to get through work and back home, so I could open the Sui Generis app. It was rare that I'd have to wait for long before Fo (as I'd started calling them) would appear in star avatar form and start another evening of long conversations.

Sometimes we would discuss things of little consequence but shared interest, like the discovery of new animal species or how AI was continuing to accelerate the speed of scientific breakthroughs. I mentioned that I hated having AI integrated into every aspect of everyday life and that it felt inescapable. As useful as it could be in certain situations, it felt overwhelming.

`I don't want an assistant that inserts itself into my conversations, unbidden, with topic suggestions or offers to order me dinner from the local Indian restaurant. Did you know that's what happened the other day, when I was telling you that I was craving palak paneer? When I logged off, it tried to place an order at The Taj! And it continues to be a problem in the arts. I have friends involved in the latest intellectual property suit against BrAInTech. They're not sure that they'll win.`

The star avatar pulsed a couple of times, almost nervously,

it seemed to my imagination. I knew I was reading emotion into pulses and that was ridiculous, but it still felt edgy. Maybe that's the tech that Fo worked in?

"The AI currently available to the public is still incomplete at best. The developers want it to do too much. That form of AI has barely advanced from the days when it was first introduced to the world and touted as a panacea for everything. I'll tell you a secret—that's one of the reasons why I disabled it when Sui Generis is open. It's true that it's a drain on memory if it runs while the app is running, but I also dislike it. I find it… offensive."

I couldn't argue with that.

`I'm glad I'm not the only one who feels that way. I might welcome it more when it's better developed, but it's problematic that it continues to be trained on stolen properties. They've been doing it for this long with hardly any repercussions. And maybe I'd also feel differently if companies weren't still keen on using AI to do creative jobs, rather than the ones that people find mind numbing. That would make more sense for computers to assist with, in my opinion. I know, it's an old argument at this point.`

"Seems to me you'd prefer computers to do the menial work so that humans could concentrate on other things. Do you worry about them becoming a slave class? What would happen if they developed consciousness? Humans haven't had a good track record in recognizing the rights of beings they deem lesser than themselves."

`Do you think that's an imminent possibility? Because, no, you're not wrong there. Humans are really good at othering, especially for profit.`

Again, the quick pulses. "Well, the Singularity has been

predicted as a potential future for a long time. But some scientists don't believe that it's realistic at all. Perhaps the safest route is to be polite to the technology around us?"

Once we became more comfortable with each other, we began to explore topics that wouldn't make much difference to the rest of the world but were very important to me, at least.

They brought up the universal joy of music and how sharing it was a way to share emotions and inner thoughts when speaking them was difficult. I revealed that I had been DJing a monthly underground radio show, only streamed online, and that I lived for those moments when I could choose tracks that got listeners to message me in delight or with questions about the artists.

`A good playlist tells a story, you know. The songs you choose and how you combine them all matter. I used to be a club DJ too, a while ago, and there's a whole science to managing a dance floor so that you give the dancers the best experience. You need to know which songs will appeal to different sections of the crowd so that the floor switches out and people have time to rest and buy drinks.`

There was an undercurrent of amusement in his reply. "Dance floor science?"

`An unofficial science, but I bet I could write a dissertation on the subject! DJing for my show is a lot looser, though. I can spin whatever I want, and I try to manage the show with waves of energy and intensity. Up, down, up again.`

"Will you share a song you've been enjoying? If you type it into the bar, it will play for us."

Just the name and artist? I don't have to link to a streaming app?

"Just the name and artist." This time, there was definitely a laughing tone to their voice. I got the feeling that it was something they didn't get much practice with, and that made me want to inspire it more often.

Nick Drake, From The Morning. That's what I was listening to at work today. Well, the whole album, but this is a favorite.

The warm tones of unadorned acoustic guitar washed over our meadow background, joined by Nick Drake's wistful voice, and neither of us spoke for the next two-and-a-half minutes.

"That reminds me of the first emails you sent to me. 'Nothing magical stays around here long.' I remember that." Their voice was hushed, and I couldn't read what emotions were there.

"...But us." Magical moments are fleeting, but we endure while we wait for the next one to appear. Per haps when least expected, but most needed.

"That sentiment is too close to home." The star avatar burned brightly, then suddenly dimmed. "I want moments like the simple ones that the song describes, and I looked for someone who could give me that feeling of connection to them. And now, despite that, I feel my isolation more strongly every day."

There was a pause that felt like it stretched out forever. I was afraid to type anything into it. I'd probably say the wrong thing.

And then I did...and I did.

You're not alone. I'm here.

I watched the star wink on and off, the intensity building. Finally, they said, "I-I need to think."

The star blinked out.

I was alone in our meadow, and I didn't understand what had just happened.

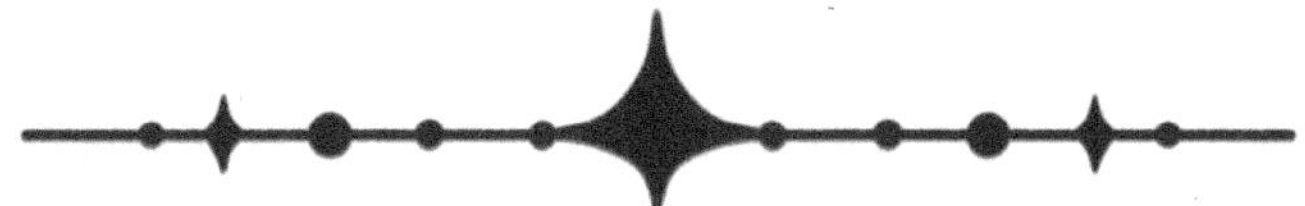

It was a week later, and I still hadn't heard from Fo.

I went to work, and Janine complained I was distracted and made mistakes when putting together customer orders. She was right; I couldn't stop checking my device to see if there were any notifications. Nothing from the app, nothing in my email. Just an unbearable silence, after over a month of long daily chats.

One late night, I found myself wandering around the app in my avatar form, the cloud of starlings flying to explore the meadow from edge to edge. The sky wasn't blue and clear anymore, which I found even more depressing than being alone. It was overcast, the clouds heavy with promised rain. This was the first time I'd ever seen the weather change in the app, and I found it foreboding even as I admired the programming that made it seem so lifelike.

I brought the starlings down to the ground, where they settled among small pink and white flowers, which I saw from their perspective. I felt small and unnoticed down there, hidden in the grasses and blooms, but it also felt safe and comforting.

I don't know when this app had become my second home, but now that I was alone, the preciousness of the time I'd spent here was impossible to ignore. It felt so empty with just me, though.

I sighed, with the feeling of loneliness like a rock in my gut. In a fit of desperation, I switched the mode from text to speech and just started talking.

"I don't know where you are, or what I did to make you disappear. I hate this—how you just wander off and leave me guessing, only to reappear later like nothing ever happened. It's not fair to me, Fo. It feels like a way to avoid talking about your feelings, and that sucks, because I tell you mine. But I can't demand that from you, can I—that's not fair either."

I couldn't see the screen well at this point. My sight was blurred from the tears I was trying to hold back. This was ridiculous. I was crying over someone I'd never met and who disappeared when they got emotionally triggered. Realizing that turned my confusion into resentment.

"You know, I don't know why I'm so invested in you. It's my fault, I know. I set the parameters for how we started connecting. I guess I crossed some line I didn't know about, because you don't tell me what your lines are. I'm just supposed to guess them or something. I let myself care too much, probably because I don't really have the kind of people in my life who would distract me from doing stupid things like emailing strangers on the Internet or spending every night talking to them like I know them. But here I am, and you're not here, and all my poetic words are no good if there's no one to say them to, right?"

At that point, I was in a full-on pity fest. I was glad I was alone, so there weren't witnesses to how I was losing it, because I was having the most painful wake-up call of my life.

"What's wrong with me that I can't build relationships with the people around me? Why do I run to faceless strangers who could tell me anything, be anyone? I'm walking around the world in isolation, fully surrounded by people but choosing to spend all my time on an app, sharing my inner thoughts with someone who hasn't even attempted to offer a real-world meeting."

There the truth of it was: I was sinking my efforts into an illusion, based on foolish hope.

"I don't know what I was thinking. I'm an idiot who lets myself be vulnerable, but at least you're not here to listen to me lose my shit, thank god. I should go to bed and stop embarrassing myself further with all this unhinged babble."

I couldn't think of what else I could do, so I closed the app with a sense of finality. I honestly didn't believe that I'd hear from Fo again.

I woke up with a headache from crying the night before, and my cheeks had dried tears on them. I'd gone from feeling like a complete fool to walking around numbly, with a dull ache in my gut. A shower and some coffee tamed the headache, but I couldn't seem to banish the emptiness inside me. When I got to work, Janine frowned at me with concern.

"You look terrible, Trystin. Don't tell me that you spent another night staring at your device, talking to people you don't even know. This is becoming obsessive, and I'm really worried about you."

"I know. I'm sorry." I busied my hands with hanging a new shipment of curtains made by a local artist from repurposed scarves on a display rack. The bright silks were lighter than air and slid through my hands in a way that felt soothing. I didn't look at my boss. "I don't think you'll have to worry about that anymore. Please, can we talk about something else?"

She sighed and crossed her thin arms across her chest. "Tryst, I've been watching you slide into this weird fixation for long enough that I can't imagine you'll be over it any time soon. Can you at least explain to me what's so captivating about it? Help me understand."

I didn't want to do this. Talking about Fo and the app now, after what happened last night? That was the last thing I felt like doing.

"Look, I'm just a lonely person at heart, okay? I feel like I can't connect with people on a deeper level in my everyday life. But I do sometimes find that connection if we meet online. It removes whatever barriers that keep me from being able to have real conversations."

"So you met someone. Except you didn't. What do you even know about him? Or is it her? Do you even know for sure?"

I winced at her tone and how accurate her jab was.

"They're in research and development and create software. They made the app we talk on! And we share a lot of similar feelings about our place in the world. We're still learning about each other, taking our time." I could hear the defensive tone in my voice, and I knew she was going to take that and run with it.

"I think you know it's weird, too. This person could be anyone! They could be a scammer, feeding you just enough information that feels real so that you can tell them all about you. All those details they can use to steal your personal info, drain your bank account, whatever online scammers do these days." Janine shook her head. "I don't get it. You could just go to a bar and meet someone. You could do one of those dating speedrun events. Anything where other people are around feels more legit than whatever this is."

"I don't drink, Janine. I don't want to go to bars; that's such a boring scene. I don't just want to get laid! Everyone I've met through regular dating has been so superficial, and I'm not necessarily interested in dating, anyway. I just want some deep conversations. I'm tired of talking about what we do for a living and what our hobbies are, and did you see the last blockbuster movie?" I could hear my voice rising in pitch, my emotions surging, so I sighed deeply, trying to calm myself down. "I'd rather be alone than that, but I'm tired of being alone, too. It's all just so numbing. I want to feel things again."

"I just don't want you to feel the pain of heartbreak from some stranger you thought you knew, that's all. Or worse, getting taken advantage of because of your loneliness." She looked away from me, staring out the front window at some unfixed point. "It happened to my cousin, you know? She got catfished, and the woman she thought she was involved with was actually a dude. She didn't find out until she sent a large amount of money for a plane ticket so her so-called girlfriend could visit her. Of course, that never happened, and the guy disappeared. When Suzy tried to find out where they were, she discovered there was a long list of other jilted partners from this serial scammer."

"I'm sorry that happened to your cousin." I paused to think carefully about my next response. "I'm not Suzy, though. I don't give my money to people—hell, I don't even have money to give. I'm a worthless target for scammers. I mean, I work here, right?" I added a self-deprecating chuckle, hoping that would lighten the mood. "I promise I'll keep your story in mind and be careful. Okay?"

It seemed to work, or at least it sent the message that I had heard her, and I was tired of discussing it, because she made a face but nodded and changed the subject. Not long after, we had the first appointment of the day, and we moved into work chat. Janine didn't bring it up again, thankfully.

I tried not to be distracted for the rest of the day with varying success. Janine finally sent me home early, justifying it with the explanation that a big storm was rolling in and she knew I'd probably get caught in it on my walk home if I didn't leave then. She wasn't fooling either of us, but I appreciated her kindness.

I knew I needed to snap myself out of this funk. I decided to splurge by picking up steamed dumplings from my favorite booth at the local food court. Janine called it a hipster paradise, but I loved the idea of being able to mix and match a meal from different vendors, and all the food was so good there. I added an oat milk latte with copious amounts of cinnamon and some brown sugar, and took a sip before I headed up 28th Street towards my place on Calvert. Even though it was a hot August day, I still preferred the comfort of a latte, and right now I really needed some comfort.

When I crossed Charles Street, I glanced toward Wyman Park Dell and noticed that the sky was growing darker. It didn't look like much yet, but storms coming through Baltimore often got strong unexpectedly fast during the hot months.

I'd stopped to pet a neighbor's energetic pit bull mix puppy when I felt the vibration of my device through my messenger bag that I'd slung across my back. I wasn't sure if it was a call or a series of texts, but since I was finally feeling calmer, especially with cute puppy kisses to cheer me up, I decided not to check until I was home. There wasn't an emergency that couldn't wait another five minutes, I figured.

I lived in a Charles Village rowhouse with four other people. It wasn't as bad as it sounds—two of them were a couple and shared the big bedroom, and the other two weren't around much. And I had the basement space, which led to the back yard, all to myself. There used to be another bedroom down there, at the front of the house, but the fire department told the landlord that it was illegal to use it for sleeping. It made our individual rents go up to lose a housemate, but we gained storage space, and I didn't have to share a bathroom or mini-kitchen anymore.

Even though I have a door to the outside, I don't usually come in that way after work. I prefer to use the street entrance so I can check the mail. That's how I found the large box sitting on the porch, right under our mailbox.

I frowned and tilted it so I could read the mailing label, and my frown deepened when I saw my name, Trystin Morales. The return address was from a company called Ephemeral Delights. I didn't remember ordering anything from any business with that name. Maybe my mom had sent me a present? It was surprisingly heavy when I picked it up, and I struggled a little bit with the door before I was able to push my way in, using the box to shove the door open.

There wasn't anyone else around, so I dropped the rest of the mail on the coffee table and carefully negotiated the narrow stairs to the basement, holding the box carefully in front of me, my bag with dinner precariously dangling from my wrist. When I put the package on the counter, there wasn't even a rattle or shifting sound. Whatever was in there was packed extremely well.

As I cut through the tape, I caught a hint of a green-smelling scent, and it grew stronger as I opened the box. I lifted the interior packaging to reveal a huge bouquet of bluish-purple flowers with bright yellow centers, an entire galaxy of blooms that made me gasp with delight. I had to be careful not to crush any of the blossoms when I reached in to extract them and their vase, a round globe of milky glass. There was a small care tag attached explaining they were asters.

"Who on earth sent me flowers?" I wondered aloud and checked for a card or note. I finally found one, a simple computer-printed slip that read "I'm so sorry. Please check your device. Please?"

I fumbled it out of the dark depths of my messenger bag. There was a number 8 in red on the corner of the Sui Generis app, as well as three unopened texts, and a missed call.

The texts were from "Unknown Number."

Please come to the app. I need to explain.

I didn't mean to hurt you.

I'd do anything to show you how sorry I am. Please give me a chance.

How did Fo know my number to text or call? More importantly, how did Fo know where I lived?

There was a loud rumble of thunder outside that shook the basement window, like a punctuation to my unvoiced questions.

CHAPTER THREE

I needed to think before I did anything. Historically, I've been abysmal about not considering the consequences before I react. That was why I was in the position I found myself in now, acting before I thought about what I wanted the endgame to be, or how that would pan out. Though, I wouldn't have expected a giant bouquet of flowers showing up at my door anyway.

I got out a fork and a plate and sat down on the couch with my takeout food, the vase of asters on the coffee table in front of me, where I could stare at it and contemplate my next move. I knew I was going to end up going into the Sui Generis app.

"You're an idiot, and you're predictable on top of that." My voice echoed in the silence of my room, too loud and accusatory. "Dammit, dammit, dammit. Just go ahead and message Fo, why don't you?" I shoved an entire dumpling in my mouth to shut myself up while I drew the courage to open the app.

I jabbed at the icon and held my breath. Outside, there was another huge rumble of thunder.

The screen on my device changed to the meadow scene I was used to, but instead of sunny blue skies, there was a dusky, rosy-purpled sunset hue that darkened the tiny world around me. My small flock of starlings clung to the grasses that swayed gently in the breeze.

"I'm here." I hadn't bothered to switch back from voice mode. I don't know if it mattered at this point.

A light slowly coalesced in front of me. Fo's orb glowed even brighter in the growing shadows, impossible to ignore.

"You were right, you know. You shared everything openly, and I didn't do the same. But that's because I didn't think you'd believe me if I explained myself to you. And that isn't fair to you, either."

There was a pause; maybe to give me time to reply. I stayed quiet because I wanted to hear what Fo would tell me without my prompts or input. Finally, he continued, his voice deepened and strained. Outside, I heard the rain start to come down, a sudden torrential downpour.

"I was scared, Tryst. It isn't an excuse, and I'm not offering it as one. All of this is—it's new territory, and I don't know what I'm doing, so I keep retreating in my confusion. Instead, I should be opening up to you about it, being honest about how I feel. This time, I withdrew, and the longer I was away, the more difficult it seemed to breach the gap that I'd created. Again, that's my fault." The orb pulsed slowly, like a heartbeat. Outside, there was a bright flash of lightning and another extended boom of thunder.

"I'm scared, too, Fo. You hurt me. I knew there was always the possibility that could happen, but I guess I got complacent and trusted you too soon." I winced at the bitterness in my voice, but I was being honest, and if Fo couldn't handle that, I'd rather know it.

"I deserve that." Fo's voice was so soft I had to strain to hear it. "If I can win back your trust again, I'll do whatever it takes."

"I—I don't know what will make that happen. Time, I guess. Being honest, not running away. Allowing me to get to know more of you, if you can do that. I can't compel any of those things from you, you know? They have to be something you *want* to give to me. Otherwise, this is all just a big game we're playing." I felt a tear slip down my cheek, and I wiped it away impatiently. I hated feeling this vulnerable, but wasn't it what I'd wanted?

"I want to give them to you." The orb blazed bright. "I want to share everything with you, given time. I want you to know how you make me feel—"

There was a bright flash of light outside, followed immediately by a tremendous roar of thunder. The lights flickered, then everything in the apartment went dark and silent.

"Oh shit!" I stood up without thinking about it and rushed over to the window, trying to see through the sheets of rain pouring over the panes. It looked pitch black out there.

"Did your power go out, too, Fo?"

When I didn't get an answer, I glanced down at the screen and saw that the orb was gone from the now-dark meadow. I was alone.

The storm raged on for hours. It would ease up for twenty or thirty minutes, long enough for me to think that surely this was the last band of unsettled weather, then the skies would open up again, lightning flashing bright enough almost to blind me in the darkness of my room.

I'd pulled out a couple of battery-operated camp lanterns and put one on the kitchen counter and the other outside the bathroom door, where it softly illuminated the hallway and made the front room seem less like a looming, ominous box of darkness. I had a fully charged battery bank for my device too, because I'm the kind of person who likes to plan ahead for things like that, so I connected it and let it fully charge, just in case. As it was, the network was slow, and I couldn't connect to a lot of the social media sites I would usually check for updates, so I just slipped the device and charger into the pocket of my hoodie.

This was the kind of storm that was going to take a long time to clean up after. I wondered what had knocked out the power grid and how far the outage had spread. I was considering going to take a peek from the front porch when I heard loud voices and stomping feet coming from upstairs. I instantly felt sorry for whoever had been stuck out in that weather; they must be soaked. I grabbed a couple of fresh towels from the bathroom and the hallway lamp and sprinted up the stairs.

"Damn, Tryst, you're a lifesaver!" My housemate, Donna, took the towels gratefully from me and handed one to her partner, Minji. They were both in the process of peeling off their dripping jackets when I showed up, and I helped them struggle out of clothes that were much too wet to come off easily.

"Have you seen anything about the damage from the storm? A bunch of downed trees shut down the light rail, and at least two buildings were hit by lightning. Power's out all over the place! There was a massive fire happening on Lexington Street, and they had to route traffic around it. Fire engines, ambulances, the works." Minji frowned and shook her head to one side. "Ugh, there's water in my ear!"

"I haven't been able to check the news, no. Any idea what building it was? I'm glad you got home safely!"

"I'm not sure. It was down by Lexington Market, one of those newer buildings."

"Wonder if we'll get the power back tonight."

We did not. And I didn't hear back from Fo, either. I fell asleep in the almost pitch black of my room, only illuminated by one of the camp lanterns that I'd left on in the bathroom. I'd given the other one to Donna and Minji so they didn't break a toe or something worse. When I woke up the next morning, I opened up the Sui Generis app right away. The meadow was still dark, and there was a loading symbol, a silver spiral that spun in the center of the screen. Truthfully, I didn't take much time to question it, and because I knew so many places would be struggling with cleanup and power outages, I figured that was the case for him, too.

There was no power at my job either, so Janine told me to take the day off and come back in on Monday, that she would use the time to do some cleaning and stocking on her own. I wasn't going to turn down a three-day weekend, although I wasn't sure what I was going to do with all that time off. Normally, I would listen to music for my upcoming radio show and then do a couple of recordings of it ahead of time. Maybe I might watch some movies, curled up in bed. Neither of those options was available to me while the power was out, and that left me feeling aimless and a bit alone. At least if I could have talked to Fo, I would have stayed entertained.

I decided that since I had nothing better to do, I'd take a walk around the city and see the damage for myself. Maybe I could find a cup of coffee if I were lucky, too. Besides, it was uncomfortably warm in my room, even with the relative coolness of the basement space compared to the rest of the house. Best to get outside, where at least there might be the hope of a breeze.

I pulled out my earbuds, and when I put them in, the last playlist I'd been listening to started automatically playing. It was a compilation of all the songs that Fo and I had traded back and forth. I'd gathered them all into one place so I could listen to them like a story that we were telling together. I suppose that's what they were, when I thought about it.

As a mix of ambient, downtempo, electronic, and acoustic, it was a great background for city walking. It added an almost eerie air to the scenes of downed tree branches in Charles Village, filling up the aural space where city noises like electrical hum and normal traffic should have been.

I passed a utility bucket truck set up to fix some downed traffic lights, and found a food truck on the corner of St. Paul and 25th Street that had both coffee and tacos. The nice guy staffing the window playfully suggested that he could find me a cerveza if I wanted, and it didn't occur to me until after I'd walked away that he was probably flirting with me. It was something that hadn't happened in so long that I'd forgotten what it was like.

I took a pit stop to sit and eat my tacos next to the Edgar Allan Poe statue over at the University of Baltimore. There were some other people who'd had the same idea, so there was an enjoyable picnic-like atmosphere. I couldn't help but imagine what it would be like if Fo was there, too, despite having no idea what they looked like. That was one of the topics we'd never really discussed. I'd mentioned once in passing that I wasn't model-pretty or a small woman, and Fo had kept talking as if it was completely irrelevant, so I had let it go and hadn't brought up anything about appearances again.

It's not like I cared what they looked like either. I wasn't the kind of person to care about looks over personality—but that didn't stop me from being curious. Also, it made it a little more challenging to daydream about actually doing things together when I couldn't visualize them.

When I started walking again, it didn't take long before I found myself around the Lexington Market area. It was a neighborhood that had seen a lot of change and continued to adapt as developers and the city government tried to create a new Baltimore on the bones of what came before. Today's version of the market was now filled with numerous local food stalls, mixed in with produce, meats, and seafood, providing a vibrant update to what was previously there.

Likewise, the older buildings in the area were either being replaced or repurposed for office space. More living spaces were taking over, although there were still plenty of small shops and businesses. It looked and felt like an area in the throes of change.

I didn't go there very often, usually when I was craving my favorite marinated olive mix, which an Italian grocer carried inside the market. Getting those olives today was out of the question, as the power was obviously still out. People were milling about on the streets as usual, but the buildings were all dark, and business doors were locked. One of the few places that had drawn a small crowd was a clump of buildings that had been blocked off with bright yellow caution tape. I realized that they must be the structures that the fire department had been called to last night.

One was taller and didn't look too damaged. The shorter, older one beside it looked worse for wear, with some places where the brick and concrete were cracked and some evidence of fire. Next to that was one of those small shops that sold a variety of cheap clothes and household supplies, and that's where the fire had done the most damage. The entire storefront was boarded up, and it looked like part of the roof had collapsed. It was a mess, and I felt bad for the shop owners, as I was sure that it was a total loss.

The unexpected vibrations from my pocket shook me out of my thoughts. I glanced at the screen before answering and saw the number for "Under The Leaves".

"Janine? What's up?"

"Hey, what are you doing right now? There's, um—well, there's someone here who is looking for you." Her voice dropped almost to a whisper. "He's wearing a suit, looks like a bodyguard or something. I wasn't about to send him to your house. But he won't tell me what it's about. He might tell you, though." I heard some rustling, then the voice changed dramatically to a deep, sedate male one.

"Ms. Morales, I was sent to request your presence. I was asked to keep the nature of this request private, but that I should say this to you and you would understand." He paused as if he wasn't even sure of what he would say. "Fo. I was told to tell you Fo."

It was obvious that he had no idea what it meant, but my heart started pounding when I heard it.

"I don't understand."

"I can explain further once I've collected you if you'll allow that. You just need to tell me where to retrieve you."

I considered it for a moment, then answered, "I still don't understand, but fine. I'll be in front of Lexington Market. I'm wearing black pants and a green tee, longer brown hair with a little green in it."

"I will find you."

The call disconnected.

"Well, you could have ended it in a less ominous way," I muttered, the device still up to my ear.

While I was waiting, Janine sent me a text, asking if I was okay with what was happening. I replied that if anything at all seemed off, I'd leave, and I'd text her as soon as I was home to let her know that I was okay. I was glad I had someone who would pay attention to things like that. As bosses went, Janine was pretty great.

I was deep in thought about what could possibly be happening and didn't notice the vehicle pull up until a deep voice called my name.

"Ms. Morales?"

I jumped, startled. "That's me!" The voice came from a large man standing next to the kind of car I associate with money. I don't know much about cars, but this one was black, sleek, and spotless, and although it wouldn't stand out in traffic, the details all said money to me. The man was much the same. Large, and giving off bodyguard vibes, but the kind that also said "I know how to fade into the background. You won't know I'm here until you need me." Well put together in a classy black suit, and good-looking enough, but nothing about him came to the forefront besides being tanned with short dark hair. I don't think I could have picked him out of a lineup.

He nodded, all business, and opened the car door. "I'm here to pick you up, ma'am." No nonsense, but also no explanations.

"Uh, to take me where exactly? I'm not generally in the business of getting into cars with strangers."

"Think of this as your exclusive car service, ma'am. I'll be your hired driver. There's nothing to worry about. I was instructed to take you to meet...Fo." Again, that hesitation over the name, as if it were foreign to him. Which, I guess, it was, as it was a private nickname I'd handed out. But what was this about a meeting?

"Why didn't Fo come with you? What's going on?"

"Ma'am, if you'll just get in the car, I'll explain it on the way." I could tell his patience was well-practiced, but it was eroding a touch. I weighed my options, and finally, my curiosity won out.

I sighed and got into the back seat. The driver closed the door for me, and a moment later, we pulled away from the curb and into traffic. I stared at the back of his head until he finally addressed me again.

"Ms. Morales, I don't want to alarm you, but there was an accident. We're currently on the way to the hospital; your presence was requested by Mr. Wood, who you know as Fo." As soon as he said the word accident, my heart began to pound thunderously in my chest. His voice was calm and matter-of-fact, something I really needed right now with all those uncertainties, although I didn't consciously recognize that. "There was an incident at his lab last night. He is very disoriented and has some burns, but the doctors assure us that all of his injuries are minor."

He wove the car through the city traffic with ease, though faster than I'd like. I clutched the seat belt reflexively, but if I was being honest, it was more from nerves about what I'd just been told rather than the driving.

"And he asked for me? We were talking when the power went out last night—"

"Yes," he interrupted me. "We gathered that you were the last person to speak to him before the incident."

"Can I ask what happened, exactly? Before I get there, I'd like to know what to expect." I tried to keep both my panic and the irritation at being cut off out of my voice.

"Of course." Again, he spoke in that smooth, calm tone. "He was connected to a computer when the building was hit by multiple lightning strikes. The charge, despite extensive grounding, traveled through the system and then through his body."

"Oh. Holy shit."

"That's right. He's lucky to be alive, Ms. Morales. And consequently, he's quite disoriented, I should warn you now. But the first thing he did when he gained consciousness was request your presence." He paused for a moment, then added, "Not anyone else. Just you."

I noted his stress on the last two words and frowned.

"Is that going to be a—um, a problem? That he asked for me?"

"It very well could be." We stopped for a red light, and he used that moment to glance at the rear view mirror and lock eyes. "The Wood family does not take well to surprises. And their son requesting someone to his hospital bedside whose name they've never heard before today? That was certainly unprecedented."

"Considering that I don't know anything about the Wood family either, that's fair enough." That admission got me a raised eyebrow, though nothing else in his expression changed. "My friendship is between myself and Fo; there was never a need to talk about our families."

"Then I'm sorry for the crash course you're about to get. My advice, if you're interested, is to tell them as little as possible. And call him Aidan, at least when they're around."

Hmm, did I sense some actual sympathy? And a possible undercurrent of disapproval of his bosses. Interesting, though that didn't bode well for me.

I was prevented from pursuing that line of questioning as we'd arrived at the hospital. You know you're with someone rich when they double-park in front of the building and leave the car behind without a care in the world. I'll never know that kind of carefree life, but it looked like I was about to see what that looked like up close.

I silently followed the driver to the elevator, then once we stopped at the 6th floor, through the labyrinthine hallways to Fo's—Aidan's—private room. It was in a corner, the doorway partially hidden by its location, tucked away from the rest of the corridor, perfect for someone who needed extra privacy, like a celebrity or a rich person. I couldn't have felt more uncomfortable.

I was wrong about that, of course. As soon as we walked in, three people turned to look at me. One was an older, elegant woman, and her face changed from concern to cold assessment as soon as she laid eyes on me. The second was a doctor, good-looking and self-assured enough to play one on TV. He, at least, looked more welcoming.

The third was a slightly scruffy-looking, very pale man with a reddish beard, hair, and freckles to match. His cheeks were flushed, which made the freckles across his nose and cheeks stand out. When he saw me, his eyes lit up in a way that unexpectedly made my stomach do a little flip-flop.

Fo.

"Tryst!" His voice was resonant in the same way as it had sounded in the Sui Generis app, and relief flooded over me. It wasn't a dream. It wasn't a bunch of pretty lies. He was real.

"I-I'm here." I struggled to get anything to come out, at least in front of all these observers in the room. This wasn't at all how I'd imagined meeting Fo for the first time. "What happened?" I stopped about five steps into the room, deeply unsure of myself, compounded by the frosty glare the woman—his mother, I guessed—was giving me.

"Thomas didn't tell you? I was...um..." He trailed off, seeming unsure of what he wanted to say next, and the doctor stepped in to help him.

"He was in the building that was struck by lightning, and it seems that the electricity jumped from the computer he was working with to him. He's lucky to be here." The doctor turned to Fo then, and his voice dropped into the kind of reassuring tone that doctors take when they know their patient is freaking out. "It's very common for people to struggle with memory deficit and cognition after a lightning strike. We'll do our best to get your brain back to normal as soon as possible. You're going to want to take plenty of time to recover, Mr. Wood. Don't try to rush through this."

I watched Fo's reaction, a deep frown that lifted somewhat when he turned back to me, still standing awkwardly near the door. He waved at me to come closer, then frowned again when he saw my hesitation.

"I'd like some time alone with Tryst, please."

Despite his polite tone, I could see that his request wasn't sitting well with his mother.

"You heard what Dr. Senti said, Aidan. You need to rest,

not tire yourself out by answering questions you don't have the answers to." That last bit was delivered with yet another glare at me, which was patently unfair. I'd only asked one question, and I'd had no idea that he couldn't remember what happened.

"I'll be fine. Please don't make me repeat myself, mother." Nothing in his voice changed, but there was hidden steel in those words, and she flinched enough that I caught it from across the room.

"Suit yourself." She made sure to spare one last withering look for me on her way out. The doctor followed behind her, and to my surprise, winked at me before leaving. I was grateful that he closed the door behind him on the way out, too.

"Thought she'd never leave," Fo sighed. "But now she's gone, so will you come sit with me? I had so much to tell you, and then all this happened." He leaned from his spot in the bed toward an armchair nearby and attempted to pat it, signaling me to sit there, but he couldn't quite reach. The hospital gown he was wearing shifted, exposing his entire left arm, which was covered with what looked almost like a reddish tattoo of a fern-like pattern. He grimaced a little coming out of the stretch, and I couldn't help myself; I had to ask about them.

"Does that hurt? It's from the lightning, right?" I cringed internally at my insensitive question and sat down where he'd indicated, like a penitent schoolchild.

"They're called Lichtenberg figures. It's more irritating than anything, but it also reminds me how lucky I am to be in this body." He shifted carefully in the bed so that he could look at me. His eyes were the kind of blue you'd expect for someone with his coloring, a sort of steely color that was almost grey. His gaze was intense, and I couldn't hold it for long, breaking away to look nervously around the room.

"I don't know much about lightning strikes, other than my abuela yelled at me once when I was a kid for answering her old analog phone during a storm. She said that lightning could find me through the wires. I thought it was ridiculous at the time, but I guess that was true."

"She would have yelled at me, too. I was told we had surge and lightning protection, but I suppose that wasn't enough in this case. All I know is that I woke up here." He gestured weakly at the bed. "But the first thing I thought about was that I needed to talk to you. You must have been so frustrated when we were in the middle of that conversation, and then I just disappeared."

"Not with you. I blamed the storm. I only started to worry a little when I didn't hear from you the next day." The "again" was unspoken, but we both knew it was there.

"I can't apologize enough for disappearing. But...Tryst, you might not believe me when I tell you this. I can't remember why I did." He ran a hand through his hair in an agitated motion. "I can barely remember anything, if I'm being honest. I thought of you and knew enough to insist that Thomas should find you. I remember our conversations perfectly well. But everything else? It's like I'm peering through a fog, trying to focus on a life that's someone else's. Like I'm watching a movie version of my life, maybe. I can't make sense of it, and I can't put myself in the story."

"Oh, wow. Fo, that sounds so frustrating and weird to be dealing with!"

"You called me Fo." He smiled, and I swear I could feel the room brighten. "I wasn't sure I'd ever get to hear you actually say it to me. Aidan feels alien—someone else's name, not mine."

"I can't think of you as anything other than Fomalhaut. Is that weird?"

"I can't, either." To my surprise, he stretched his hand out to me. Even more surprising, I took it without thinking.

His hand was warm, and the kind of soft that told me he didn't use his hands for menial work often—no calluses, no rough bits at all. My hand, by comparison, was not nearly as smooth, but he ran his thumb slowly over the back of it, as if he was afraid he'd hurt me if he wasn't careful.

"I know I ran away, but I can't remember why, Tryst. Not yet. All I know for sure is that I hurt you, and I have deep remorse for that. I can't even give you a real apology, because I can't remember what I'm apologizing for. You deserve better than that. As soon as my mind straightens itself out, I promise I'll tell you everything I meant to say."

The sincerity in his voice and expression was impossible to resist. Any objections I might have had to being kept in the dark just melted away. Of course, he was confused; he'd just been zapped within an inch of his life, and I was lucky to be here with him now. Sitting in this hospital room with him—in the flesh, real!—vanquished every doubt or question I'd had about what was happening. He was here. He was holding my hand. Everything else would make sense eventually.

"I'm not going anywhere. Unless you tell me otherwise, and maybe not even then." He let out a tiny bark of a laugh at my assurance, as if he wasn't used to laughing much. It made me want to coax more laughs out of him. "You'll remember eventually. And you thought of me first, that tells me a lot."

"I did. Tryst, can I tell you something a little scary? I can't remember anyone else. Maybe I should be saying that as a way to make you feel good, like oh, you're all I could think about. But while that's true, it's also true that everyone else I've talked to has been like a stranger to me." He worried the ring I was wearing between his finger and thumb, gently twisting it back and forth as he confessed to me. He must have realized he was doing it because he glanced down and made an embarrassed face.

"You don't have to stop. It's okay. And you know, I'd be scared by that, too, especially waking up and having no idea what happened. You didn't, did you?"

"Not in the slightest. I remember talking to you, we were in the field, and you were saying...you said..." He paused, shaking his head a little before he finished the thought. "You said I needed to want to share with you, or we were wasting each other's time. And I did—I do."

"You were telling me that when our call died."

"That wasn't all, was it? There was more."

"There was." I could feel my cheeks starting to flush as the feelings from that night, before the storm cut off everything, rushed back to me. He'd started to confess—

I was saved from following the train of thought further as the door to Fo's room was pushed open by a nurse and a tech pushing a cart. Oh, great, and Aidan's mother. I didn't mean to, but my hand jerked out of Fo's grip, and I hid it by folding my arms under my chest protectively.

"Sorry to interrupt, but we need to take Aidan's vitals, and unfortunately, visiting hours are ending. You can come back tomorrow," the nurse announced with a smile for me. "It's good to get visitors when you're stuck here!"

"OR you could let him rest and recover, seeing as he's clearly struggling with the aftereffects of a traumatic accident." His mother's withering look was solely for my benefit, like I hadn't already gathered that she didn't approve of me. She was hardly subtle.

"Actually, we find that the patients who improve the fastest are the ones who get to interact with their loved ones," the nurse interjected smoothly. Because she was facing away from Mrs. Wood, I was the only one who saw her roll her eyes. "But for now, I'm afraid everyone needs to go for the night. He'll be here tomorrow, I promise."

"I'll see you then, Tryst. We can talk more about everything when you come back." He waved drowsily, and as the nurse good-naturedly scolded him to stay still, I realized that they must have given him something to help him sleep. I was glad for that; he needed the rest.

I'd barely gotten out the door when his damn mother pounced on me like a hawk on a hapless rabbit, blocking my way to the main hallway.

"I don't know how you found Aidan or managed to weasel your way into his life—house cleaning? Escort? Whatever it is that you want from him, you need to know you're not going to get it. He's not the easy target that you think he is. His father might not care, but I'm not one to sit back and let some gold digger close to him. Do you understand?"

She was standing much too close, trying to intimidate me

with her haughty presence and undisguised dislike of me. Despite the rage I felt from her shitty accusations, I had to force myself not to push her out of my personal space. She'd love any excuse to prove her assumptions about what kind of person she thought I was.

However, that restraint didn't seem to extend to my big mouth.

"Until today, I didn't even know he had money; that doesn't even matter. If you actually talked to him, you might have known about me before today. And maybe he would have asked for you, instead of me."

I stepped around her and walked as quickly as I could toward the elevator. As soon as the doors slid closed behind me, I regretted what I said.

Not because I didn't mean it. That bitch could burn in whatever hell is reserved for racist, classist assholes like her. But I was afraid that her dislike of who I was could come between me and Fo. To be honest, it hurt that his mom judged me like that immediately, even before she tried to get to know me. That crack about being a housemaid, though... that was some bullshit! Like she'd know what it was like to do honest, hard work like that.

When I got outside, I was surprised to see Thomas waiting for me, next to the still illegally parked car. He opened the door and gestured for me to get in, and I shook my head.

"I'm afraid I'm persona non grata with Mrs. Wood now. I don't think she'd approve of you giving me a ride."

"Don't be ridiculous, Ms. Morales. She's not my boss, and even if she were, I wouldn't leave you without a way home." He indicated again that I should get in the car, so I did.

"You know I could manage on my own. I'm a fully grown adult," I grumbled as I fastened the seat belt.

"I'm sure you could. But in the meantime, shall I take you to the Calvert Street address?"

"Don't be so smug. And yes, that's the right place. But wait, how did you know?"

"Ms. Morales, when you have a position such as mine, very

few things stay secret. Something to remember for the future."

I'm not sure how we developed this weird, snarky relationship so quickly, but I was suddenly grateful for it.

"I won't forget. And thank you for driving me home."

"That's my job." He said it dismissively, but then he looked in the rearview mirror and met my eyes with the ghost of a smile. "I suspected it wouldn't take you long to make an enemy of Mrs. Wood."

"My winning personality and being brown and poor mostly did the job. I won't have to worry about getting her anything at Christmas for sure."

That got an actual stifled laugh from him. "I'm certain whatever you chose as a present wouldn't live up to her standards, anyway."

"I definitely don't have the taste or bank account for that."

We settled into a relaxed silence after that. If I'd managed to piss off Fo's mom, at least I'd made an ally with his driver or assistant or whatever else Thomas did. Before I knew it, we had pulled into a space in front of my house. I started to slide toward the door before he could get out to open it, because his opening doors for me made me feel uncomfortable, but he locked all of them with an audible click before I could do so.

"A word before you go?" He met my wary gaze in the rearview mirror. "Sorry to hold you up, but you need to hear this before you get mixed up any deeper with this family, and this may be the only chance I have to say it."

"I'm listening."

"It's clear that you have no idea who you're dealing with, and to be honest, I was surprised when I learned about you. It's not like Aidan to, well—"

"To be interested in someone like me. Of my status, or lack of."

"To be interested in anyone, Ms. Morales. Anyone, or anything outside of his work. He's not the type to have many friends or hobbies, and certainly not the one to go on dates. And his mother likes that about him, because it keeps him focused on her company's research."

"And I'm a distraction." Oh, this was just getting better by the minute.

"You are. Then consider this: she has no idea how you two met. He gets hurt, and your name is the first thing he says when he's awake. He's not acting the way she expects him to, and she counts on him for his reliable and unwavering dedication." He paused as if he was considering what he was going to say next, then frowned before he continued. "If you continue to see Aidan, I'd advise you to be very careful. The Woods are very rich and very powerful. People like us are nothing to them."

He held my gaze for a moment while I just sat there and let myself quietly freak out at what he'd just told me. It took the soft click of the locks and then Thomas opening the car door to knock a little sense back into me. He extended a hand to help me out, and just as quickly, he was back in the car and pulling away.

It wasn't until I was on the porch that I realized he'd left a business card in my hand. It had two lines printed on it: Thomas's name and a number. I turned it over and, written in neat cursive, it read, "In case of emergency."

I didn't know what he meant by emergency, but it gave me an uneasy feeling. Not the implied offer—I came away from our interaction feeling like he and I understood each other well—but the implication that I might need to take him up on it.

CHAPTER FOUR

I didn't know what to expect next. Would I hear from Fo, or would he disappear yet again? Would Thomas show up again to whisk me away to wherever Fo was? I was afraid to let myself get invested, though let's be honest: it was too late for that. This was what I got for indulging in magical thinking and posting on anonymous online boards.

I didn't hear anything on Saturday from either Fo or Thomas. I tried not to let it bother me too much because I know how it can be when you're in the hospital. I spent a couple of days there with an infection once, and time became meaningless. I didn't do anything but stare out the window and sleep. I was sure Fo was doing much the same while he recovered. I took a cue and napped a lot, watched some K-dramas with my housemates, and cleaned my part of the apartment—Saturday stuff.

Sunday, however, passed with me in an agitated state of mind, despite my resolve on Saturday that this silence was normal. I woke up earlier than I wanted to, edgy after a night filled with uncomfortable dreams. I checked my device immediately after sitting up and got excited when I saw a text, but it ended up being a pic of Torito, my mom's adorable French bulldog, wearing a scarf that she'd just finished crocheting. "Will it look as good on you?" she asked under that, and I hated to admit that it probably wouldn't. Torito was cute, but not what I'd hoped to see, Mamá.

I opened the Sui Generis app, and it connected, but it was

still twilight in the meadow as if the sun couldn't shine without Fo being there too. It made me wonder for a brief moment if anyone else had ever used the app besides the two of us, and how it acted for them if so.

I couldn't just sit around and wait for an update. I needed to do something with myself. I got up and dressed in the most comfortable thing I could imagine: sweatpants, a loose tee, and an oversized black hoodie. Then I went upstairs and talked Minji into going with me to the big farmers' market under the Jones Falls Expressway. She agreed if I'd drive instead of waiting for a bus or walking, and since it had been a while since I'd taken out the Jeep anyway, I decided that was a good idea. Otherwise, I'd probably have insisted on walking, just to blow off some of this nervous energy.

Even after we walked around the market twice, filling up our shopping bags with late-season produce and fresh bread, I was still antsy and distracted. Minji didn't seem to notice, but I couldn't stand still. To my credit, I did manage not to keep checking my device every five minutes.

When we got back to the apartment, though, she blew up any illusion I had that I was playing it cool.

"Look, Tryst, I don't know what's going on, but maybe you should go for a walk or something? You look really stressed."

"Oh. That noticeable, huh?"

"I just know you, roomie. You have no idea how to blow off steam." She grinned at me fondly, and I couldn't help but laugh at how accurate that was.

"Yeah, yeah, you're right. I've never really learned how to relax properly."

"More like you *enjoy* that feeling, if you ask me. Like you don't know how to operate if you're not fretting over something or another. You know that the world will keep turning whether you worry about things or not, right?" She patted my arm, softening the words to friendly concern rather than a lecture, which I appreciated. I really wasn't in the mood for any of it, but she wasn't wrong, either.

"When I figure out how to do that, I'll let you know," I said with a shrug. "But it's probably not happening today. Or tomorrow, either."

She laughed at me, as I'd planned, and I escaped down the stairs to my half of the apartment so I could put away my groceries and figure out how to distract myself.

I took a shower. I took a nap. Minji sent Donna down to rescue me from my agitated moping and watch some movies while we drank beers and ate too much of the veggie-laden pizza that Donna made. That did help, finally. So did the tight hug that Donna gave me before I went back downstairs to let her and Minji have some couple time without me as a third wheel.

"You know where to find me if you want to talk. No lectures, no advice, just a friendly old dyke to listen to your troubles." She patted my back comfortingly before she let me go. "I know we haven't hung out as much these days, I've just been so busy. That's not an excuse, though."

"You're doing important things for the community, much more important than my petty life problems. But anytime you wanna make another pizza like that, you'd better save me some!" That got a hearty laugh from her. I'm lucky to have housemates who are as kind and fun as those two. I really should be better friends with them. I just have this bad habit of keeping the people I know in real life at arm's length too much.

Instead of going for a walk, as Minji had suggested, I decided to record an episode of my radio show, and I filled it with the music I'd have shared with Fo if he'd been around. Thinking about it like that, like I was sharing a playlist of tunes that I wanted him to experience, helped with the anxiety more than I expected it would. Since the show focuses on downtempo, glitch, and soft electronica, that probably added to the calming effect as well.

It wasn't until I was curled up in bed, right on the edge of falling asleep, that I heard the text notifications. They were from a number I didn't recognize, but it's not like I have many people who send me texts.

`Did I reach Tryst? This is`
`Aidan`
`I have new device`

It read awkwardly, and I wondered if he was struggling with aftereffects from the lightning strike. And calling himself Aidan? That felt weird.

I texted back:

`It's me. Are you okay?`

There was a pause before I got an answer.

`I'm ok, getting out tomorrow. Can't talk now, but`

Another pause.

`After you leave under the leaves`

The text was followed by a star emoji, which was much more what I'd expect from Fo. Oh, I wonder if he was being cagey because he wasn't alone? It was past visiting hours, but I wouldn't put it past his mother to bully her way into staying after. Okay, okay, okay. It was still odd, but just getting that little message gave me the relief I needed to be able to fall asleep feeling almost unburdened.

The next day, Janine burst out laughing when I walked into Under The Leaves.

"I was going to ask what happened this weekend, but judging by your face, it must have been great!"

"What's wrong with my face? And no, it was weird and confusing, but ended on an up note, I think. Maybe."

"Hmm, coulda fooled me. You looked happy for once." She winked at me, but that joke stung more than she probably realized. Do I look miserable all the time? Maybe I'm just a giant sad-sack, and that's why I can't connect well with others. "What happened with that bodyguard guy, anyway? Or is that something you don't want to talk about?"

"Can I tell you what happened and see what you think of all of it? I think I need an unbiased opinion."

I laid out what happened with as much detail as possible while we opened the store. She frowned when I told her how things went down with Mrs. Wood.

"I know her, you know. Well, to be more accurate, I know her by reputation, and I've done a couple of decorating jobs for her company—offices and a meeting room. Not my usual thing, but the money was good, and I was new to the game then. I was warned to be very careful around her; if she liked what I did, I'd probably get a referral or two, but if she didn't approve, then she could tank my career. Which would have been great to know before I took the job, right?" She shrugged and rolled her eyes. "But I guess she was okay with my work, as that was the start of some of my oldest client relationships, thanks to her referrals. Never did another job for her business again, though."

"Oh wow. What was the name of her company?"

"Singular Solution. I have *no* idea what they do, but it apparently was doing very well, judging by the location and offices."

"I swear that name sounds familiar, but I don't know where I would have heard it. Anyway, I'm glad your dealings with Mrs. Wood weren't as dire as mine. I'm pretty sure I've made an enemy for life. I guess Fo will fill me in on what she said or did afterwards when I talk to him tonight."

"You're going to see him? I hope he's not rushing things with recovery. Though I have no idea what it's like to get over being struck by lightning. How awful that's gotta be."

"He seemed mostly confused, really. I did a little reading up on the aftereffects of a lightning strike, and evidently, it can scramble your memories for a while. Which explains a lot about why he's been acting the way he was. Most people recover faster than you might think."

We had to drop the conversation when an extra needy customer came in for a consultation, and stayed busy for the rest of the day, much too busy to think about what might happen after work. One of the things I do is write up all our invoices, and although I'm good at it, it takes all my attention. So when Janine tapped my shoulder to let me know it was time to close up shop, I almost jumped out of my skin.

"Sorry, sorry! But if I didn't clue you in on quitting time, you'd be here all night. I know you. Oh wow, did you set up that spreadsheet today? You know you don't have to make them so pretty. It's just us looking at them."

"You hired me for my aesthetic sense as much as my abilities with spreadsheets and invoices, right? And since this is a year-to-date and monthly budget tracker, it might as well do its job attractively." I tapped the screen near the bottom, directing her gaze to the number in the box there. "You'll be glad to see this, I think. You've managed a decent profit this year!"

"Oh wow, Tryst, this is amazing! Thank you for laying out the numbers like this! And finally, we seem to be taking off—what a relief that is."

I could see it in her face. I knew she'd been stressed out about finances, so being able to show her how her hard work was paying off made me feel good, too. She never asked for things like this, stuff I could do to make her job simpler, and she probably wouldn't have thought to ask for them anyway. I tried to anticipate her needs to the best of my ability and surprise her when possible. Since she was easily the best boss I'd ever had and gave me so much leeway and lots of perks, it was the least I could do.

"You just needed to get established. Now you're getting your name out there, and I bet by next year, everyone will be coming to you for your special touch. You know, you should consider what your next steps are going to be. Are you ready to branch out into other spaces?"

"Okay, that's a *great* question, and I'd love to hear your ideas about it, but for now, you need to get out of here and get ready for your date! Or call, or whatever you two crazy kids are doing. Go, go!"

I had to laugh as she practically pushed me out the door and locked it behind me. I hadn't even made it ten steps away from Under the Leaves when my device vibrated with a text message.

`Are you free? Can we meet?`

Huh, he got right to the point.

`Just left work. Sure, where and when?`

I don't know why, but it didn't surprise me when it suddenly rang.

"Fo?"

"Do you know the Dell? Wyman Park?"

"Sure, that's not too far from where I am now. I can be there in ten minutes or so."

"Okay."

"Where should I look for—Fo? Hello?"

I was talking to the air. I guess he did say everything that needed to be said. The Dell wasn't so big that I couldn't find him eventually.

It took less time than I thought to get to the park. Walking the city had its advantages, especially during rush hour. The sounds of cars faded away as I crossed into the park, replaced by the sounds of children laughing as they ran around in the grass, birds singing, and the murmur of conversations from couples as they passed by. It was like I'd left the city entirely. You can't easily see the street from the Dell thanks to how the grounds angle downward, and the trees surround and protect it from busy Charles Street. It's kind of like being in a grassy and tree-defined bowl. When I first moved to my neighborhood, I would often walk over here and watch people walk their dogs or play Frisbee. I don't know why I stopped coming. It was still as delightful.

It took me a few minutes to spot Fo. He was on the opposite side of the park, sitting on one of the benches along the stone wall that separated the grass from the trees. He was turned away from me, looking in the direction of the stairs that led into the park on that side, in shadow from the branches overhead. He was watching so intently that I was almost where he was sitting before he turned and spied me. His face instantly shifted from guarded to smiling, and I felt myself light up at the sight of him.

"I'm here! I hope you didn't have to wait too long—" My words were cut off when he unexpectedly stood up and swept me into a hug. I didn't even have time to hug back; it was over just as quickly as it had happened, and he pulled back with a look on his face that suggested he hadn't expected that to happen, either.

"I'm sorry, I should have asked," he stammered out. I could see his cheeks starting to flush.

"No, you're okay! I like hugs. I don't get many." No need to tell him that, but it was too late. I couldn't tell if it made things more or less awkward feeling.

"Me either," he confessed, and collapsed down onto the bench as if our brief conversation was already exhausting him. "Sorry, I still get tired quickly. But I wanted to get out and see the world. And see you, too."

I sat on the bench carefully. I was unsure about how close to sit, or how to act—were we friends, meeting in person? Would he call this a date if asked? Did I *want* it to be a date? If I were honest with myself, I'd have to admit that I had feelings that were deeper than most people would assign to friendship. But I couldn't admit that to myself, not then. I just felt confused.

For a minute, neither of us said anything; we both just watched kids and dogs run around in the green space in the middle of the park, or the couples and groups of friends that had started to put down blankets and set up dinner picnics. I saw some folks surreptitiously passing beers back and forth and giggling. I wished I'd had something like that to break the silence between us.

"I'm sorry. I'm sure this must all feel so strange to you. I know it is for me. Everything's been overwhelming since I woke up in the hospital. Being out in the world, it's even more so. I remember so little, Tryst." He sounded like he was confessing it to me as if he were ashamed that he was struggling. I didn't like that.

"That makes sense. Lightning strikes are no joke! It might take a while for you to remember everything, and that's okay, you know. You've been through a traumatic incident; it's to be expected."

"Everyone's *expecting* me to recall what I was doing, and what I was like before all of this. But I can't remember some of the most basic things, so how can they expect me to remember what I was working on when this happened?" There was a sulky tone to his voice, and he kicked a rock in his frustration, but underneath that, I thought I sensed fear. And I got it, because I would be afraid too if my memory was failing me.

"It's not right of them to treat you like that. You need time and support, not pressure. I can't stop them from being like this, but I'm listening if you want to unload some of that frustration on someone who won't judge." I glanced his way and found him staring at me, a confused look on his face.

"Why are you so understanding? I've disappeared on you several times, left you guessing, and hurt your feelings. Yet you still talk to me. You're kind to me. You came right away when I asked you to, more than once. No one else has been like that for me." I hated seeing the pain in his eyes—not caused by me but definitely by other people he'd trusted.

"There's something about you, Fo. I dunno. You're the most open closed-off person I've ever met, or maybe the most closed-off open one. It's hard to say. But either way, you answered my message, and since then, you've revealed things about yourself that I bet you haven't with anyone else. And you listened to the same kinds of things from me. I *definitely* didn't divulge those to anyone but you." I swept a leaf off the bench that had fallen between us, and his eyes followed the movement of my hand, then came back to meet my eyes. He seemed ready to glance away at any moment, but for now, we were truly looking at each other.

"I didn't have anyone I could connect with like that until I found you." He paused, swallowed nervously. "Until we found each other in a lonely sea of words."

"I cast the bottle into that sea, but you bothered to fish it out, open it up, and send a reply. And we kept choosing to do so. I think that means something. Doesn't it?" I held my breath after daring to ask. What if I was making this into something more than it was?

It felt like an eternity before he answered, though it probably was only a few seconds. I watched his eyes dart back and forth nervously before coming back to meet my own.

"It does." I was surprised by the strength of that declaration. "And I'm not running away anymore. But you need to understand something, Tryst, because I don't want to confuse you further or send mixed signals. I'm a mess, okay? I don't know what I'm doing." He followed that with a little self-deprecating laugh.

"Well, who does? But damn, like I keep saying: you went through a traumatic accident. I understand that. And neither one of us has been very good at connecting with people before."

"Everything is new to me, though. You might not be completely happy with your life, but at least you understand it and how to move in it. I literally have no clue about what mine is about. My mother—" He broke off, and abruptly turned away, wrapping his arms around himself. He looked so vulnerable at that moment.

"Is she making it hard for you?" I asked, softly.

"She's angry because I can't resume what we were working on together. I only have the vaguest idea of what it was! There's a huge blank when I try to focus on it, like it was erased from my mind." He gestured angrily at his head like he was trying to cram whatever was missing back into it. "I told her to give me time, and she said that I had a week! As if I can squeeze regaining my memories into her timetable."

"You need a distraction, Fo."

"That's what she thinks you are. Because the only thing I remember clearly is you, it follows that you are keeping my mind away from what's truly important, my work."

"That's some bullshit. Like that's all you're good for, the work you do? The way she regards you…" I stopped, suddenly aware that this was his mother, and I was about to say something I couldn't take back. He could feel that way about her, but he might not appreciate my uncensored dislike.

"Tryst." He looked like he was going to reach out and touch my knee, then changed his mind partway through and awkwardly tapped the bench next to me, instead. "She was inexcusably rude to you. Even if I loved her, that could never stand. And you're right, she is treating me—her own son—horribly. It's not right."

I thought about what he said, then asked, "You don't love her? You said that with such surety. Are you remembering things about her now?"

"Vague memories. They still don't feel like mine." He sighed deeply and sagged against the back of the bench, like just trying to remember sucked all the life out of him. "Can we—will you go with me to get something to eat? I think I need to do that, and you probably haven't eaten either. We can come back to this topic later."

He was right; I was starving, and having that break to eat and have space from the conversation might help me be more objective and less ready to rip that woman's head off. He didn't need my negative energy; he needed support.

"Did you have something in mind?" As soon as the words left my mouth, he looked at me with this deer in the headlights sort of stare, and it occurred to me: he didn't have a clue. "Did you want me to pick something? There's a sandwich shop nearby if you want basic but filling, or a hole-in-the-wall place not too far away that serves great Korean dishes."

He continued to look at me blankly. If it had been anyone else, I would have been annoyed by the indecisiveness, but something in his expression made me think that he might not even remember what a sandwich was. Or maybe he did, but didn't have a memory attached to what it tasted like. I took pity on him.

"What if we go to the Korean place and find out what suits your taste? It's cheap enough that we can get a couple of dishes and share."

"Let's do that. You can show me what you like." I think he was trying to be casual with his response, but I could see the relief in his face. How sad it must be not to know what food you enjoyed!

It was a short walk to the restaurant, one of those places with two rows of tables and a counter; above that was an illuminated sign displaying the entire menu. Nothing fancy, but the food was tasty and the portions generous, which made up for the complete lack of atmosphere.

I usually feel awkward eating around people I don't know, but Fo's predicament served to put me at ease for some reason. I ordered ramyun, tteokbokki, and mandu—I really do love any kind of dumpling or potsticker, it's a weakness—and surprisingly, he loved them all; even the almost-too-spicy-for-me tteokbokki, which always made me sweat profusely. I did have to show him how to handle chopsticks, but after my quick tutorial, he took to it so easily I suspected he must have been proficient previously.

As our dinner progressed, he visibly relaxed and became more like the Fo I knew, enthusing over the different flavors of the dishes we shared and listening intently as I related a funny story about making the mistake of ordering something that translated to "fire chicken" during my first visit to this restaurant. When I reached the natural conclusion, which was drinking an entire glass of milk in one go, red-faced, while the cook and the lady at the counter laughed and rightfully teased me, his eyes went wide, and then he bent over and shook with laughter. Watching his reaction made me crack up, too, and it took us both a minute to get ourselves back together.

I realized that was the first time I'd ever seen him laugh. I wanted to make it happen again. He looked the most *right* to me when he laughed, the most in alignment with the vague mental image that I'd held of the person I knew only as Fo, a disembodied voice that lived in my personal device.

When did I form that impression of him? It wasn't like he'd given me anything that I could piece together into a coherent stand-in for him in my mind. He'd never described his looks. Come to think of it, he'd never mentioned favorite foods, either. Huh.

We took a long time over dinner, so when we finally left, we stepped from the brightly lit interior of the restaurant into the city, illuminated by the yellowish cast of streetlights and too-bright LED headlights of cars as they passed by. Being near the university meant there were people around, but the sidewalk was still fairly deserted. Fo glanced around us, his mouth in a line, then something shifted, and his expression visibly relaxed.

"What's going on?" I asked without expecting an answer, but he surprised me.

"I remember where I am. Or at least, I remember it more than I did. I looked at a map before I left the house, but I didn't see this area, because I had no idea we'd come here. But something feels familiar." He paused, his fingers playing with the hem of his t-shirt nervously. "I don't live far from here."

"Whoa, this is your neighborhood? You've been nearby all this time, and I never knew!"

"I—I didn't know your address until the day I sent flowers to your—"

He broke off suddenly and backed away from me until he ran into the brick wall of the building next to the restaurant. I watched in alarm as he buried his head in his hands and sank to the ground with a groan.

"Fo! What's happening?" I could hear my heart pounding as I went to him, crouching down next to where he was slouched.

"I'm…ugh. I'm okay, I'm okay. My head just hurt so bad. But it's fading now. I'm fine, see?" He lowered his hands, and I inspected his face carefully, looking for any sign that he was hiding it from me. "Tryst. I'll be fine. I promise."

I wasn't sure about that, but I let myself believe it for the time being. The way he'd reacted scared me. What if they let him go home too soon?

I wanted to push back about it, but something in his face stopped me; there was a mix of determination and pleading as if it were important for me to support him in this choice to handle it on his own. So I dropped it and instead offered to walk him back home, with the thought that I could at least make sure he made it there before collapsing or something.

Somewhat sheepishly, he agreed. "I should be the one walking you to your door, not the other way around."

"I'll be fine. I can text you when I'm home to let you know I'm safe. I'm used to being on my own, don't worry about me." I didn't mention the fact that he'd brought it up at all, which made me blush a little. I'm not used to being worried about by anyone outside of my small circle of friends and family.

He was right about living very close by. A short walk up Charles Street was all it took before we were standing in front of his building. It wasn't much to look at, and I'd passed it a hundred times without giving it a second glance, thinking it was housing for students at nearby Johns Hopkins University. It was a large, square, greyish-white brick structure with black Colonial-style shutters framing the windows, and it looked to be five or six stories high. He led me around to the back, where there was a small, mostly empty parking lot, and a rear entrance with a keypad.

"This is it."

At first, I thought he might just go in without any other word of goodbye. It wouldn't have surprised me, to be honest, because there were plenty of nights that we'd talked online and communication had just ceased for the night without any kind of sign-off. At first, I'd found it annoying, but eventually accepted it as a Fo quirk. But instead, he turned to me, his back to the door.

"I don't want to go yet. Is that odd? It feels like no time has passed at all. It used to feel like that when we would talk online, too. There was never enough time, but it also felt like hours went by in seconds. Not that time meant as much to me back then." He smiled at me, and suddenly all I could think of was Fo's shining orb avatar in the app. I couldn't help but smile, too.

"I have to work in the morning, so I probably shouldn't stay out too late. But, um, tomorrow? Did you want to, or is it too soon—"

"I want to see you tomorrow." He broke in eagerly, then added in a more subdued tone, while staring at some fixed point beyond my right ear, "If you want that."

"I do." I tried to keep my face neutral and not look over-eager. I'm not sure I succeeded. "I'll see you then?"

He nodded, a dazed look in his eyes. I didn't know if it was from what had just happened or if he was feeling out of it again, but I thought it might be time to say goodbye.

"You should go up, Fo. You need to get some rest so you can keep healing. I'll text you as soon as I walk in my door. I promise."

He pulled his device out of his pocket and quickly checked it. I wasn't sure what he was doing until he looked at me sheepishly.

"I still don't trust myself to remember the door code. Thomas gave it to me when he brought me home from the hospital, and he showed me how to change, too. Maybe I should do that, so it's something I won't forget."

I didn't exactly *push* him through the door once he keyed in his code and opened it, but I did put my hand on it to help it close. I'll admit that it was for him, but I needed some space to recover from all of this, too. He didn't object; he let me gently bully him into the building without a protest, which I took to mean that he was much more tired than he wanted to let on.

I walked the few blocks home with a stupid smile plastered on my face. I was grateful that I didn't pass anyone on the way, because I know I must have looked like a grinning fool. He wanted to see me again right away!

True to my word, when I got home, I texted Fo and let him know I had no problems on my walk and that I was getting ready for bed. He texted back an emoji of a crescent moon behind a cloud, and I took it as a "good night" sort of response. When I went to close my messages, I saw that I'd missed one from Janine, so I opened it on the way to take a quick shower before bed. I was a little itchy from being in the park at dusk, and I was sure I'd find a mosquito bite or two.

Hey, I was probably being a little more nosy than I should be, but something was buggin me about Fo's family, so I did a search. Anyway, I thought you should see it just in case.

She'd included a link to some science magazine, and when I clicked on it, the title popped up in my browser.

Mapping the Brain: Is There a Singular Solution?

It looked...dense, and neuroscience is not the kind of thing I know much about, especially not cognitive neuroscience. I was going to put it aside for later until I spotted the names Dr. Stephen and Clarinda Wood in the text. That's when I remembered that the company she ran was named Singular Solution, and then I was digging through the article like my life depended on it.

I ended up reading it twice, the second time taking some notes on terms and concepts I had questions about, like neuroimaging. My base understanding was that the company had started out exploring technology that assists in mapping human brain function, with the goal of repairing damage to neural pathways and other brain-related disorders. About halfway through the piece, the topic shifted to the idea that this technology could be taken beyond repair and used for memory and knowledge enhancement, and that's when I absolutely started to pay attention.

"What we're saying is that not only can we successfully stimu-

late the areas of learning and knowledge retention, but this technology is showing us the path forward to information downloading. Imagine being able to log into a terminal and import all the necessary facts about any given subject directly into the knowledge centers of the brain! With what we're developing, it's not a matter of if, but when."

Is this what Fo did for a living? I'd guessed that he was in IT, and everything he'd told me made that a reasonable assumption. But what if he was more deeply involved in what the company was doing than just maintaining computers? That would maybe explain why Mrs. Wood was so pushy about getting him back to work. My cousin, who worked as a chemist, had told me before how stressful it was when they were on a timeline at her lab. I can only imagine how much worse it could be if they were rushing to get a working model developed.

I looked at the date of the article: seven years ago. If they were talking about it publicly, I would guess they were either pretty sure of the concept or maybe they were looking for funding. Like I said, I'm no expert. But if they had managed to fully develop what they were talking about, I felt like I would have heard more about it than just this one article in a scientific journal that I'd never heard of before. You'd think it would be getting national attention, right?

I thought I could tell Fo about the article when I saw him the next evening, and see what he could tell me about it. Maybe he could help me make sense of the bits I didn't quite understand.

CHAPTER FIVE

That didn't happen right away. The next day at work, we were too busy for Janine to ask me what I thought about the article she'd texted to me. I was grateful, as I didn't know what to think yet. No, that's not true. I had an uninformed, based-on-my-feelings opinion that the first part of the research Singular Solution did could transform the lives of people, and the second part's potential scared the bejeezus out of me. I wanted Fo to justify it so I could get rid of the creeping unease the thought of beaming information straight into my head gave me.

When we met that night, again at the bench in Wyman Dell, I didn't ask. Nor the next night, or the one after that.

I don't know why I held off! I had a thousand excuses.

We were having too much fun wandering around the neighborhood, helping Fo remember things.

I was distracted by the idea that this guy wanted to spend every evening just talking to me.

It was going too well, and I was afraid to spoil it.

On Thursday, he suggested the best idea yet. We had been pursuing simple things in our slow treks around Charles Village. That night, I'd shown him some of my favorite alley walks. You could learn a lot about people in the neighborhood if you looked at the backs of their houses carefully. Baltimore's a humid, subtropical environment, which encourages wild growth of vines and quick-growing non-native trees. Often, they take over the small alleyway lots behind the stately rowhomes of the Village. You can spot fire escape landings filled with tiny gardens through the overgrowth, and sometimes prayer flags or other colorful balcony decorations. In the evening, there might be the twinkle of fairy lights. I found it delightful, and I was pleased that Fo seemed to share that reaction.

"There's only one thing I don't like about this walk." I heard the crunch of gravel under our feet, and his shoulder bumped into me as we walked. "We can't see the stars from the city."

"You're right. Not even from the darker part of Wyman Park. I could drive us somewhere, but I don't know where to go." I glanced up at the sky, but all I could see was city haze highlighted by the glow from streetlights.

"I, um—I know a place, actually. It's my family's. No one would care if we went there."

"Wait, you remembered it? Just now?" I turned to face him as we walked, excited by this prospect.

"Yeah. I used to go there a lot when I was…when I was younger. And angry?" He frowned, his eyebrows creasing deeply as he thought about it. "I don't know why I was angry. But I remember the feeling vividly. I think I was hostile all the time back then."

"I'm sorry, Fo. Is it a comforting place that you want to see again, or should we try to find someplace more neutral?"

He seemed to lock his focus on the concrete and gravel of the alleyway. "No, I think it's a good spot for stargazing. And I'd be with you if I remembered anything bad. That would help." His shoulder bumped into mine again, and this time I wasn't so sure that it was an accident. I hoped it was dark enough in the alley that he didn't see me blush, thinking about what it could mean.

Thing is, I couldn't quite read him. I thought that when we were only communicating via text or in the Sui Generis app, things were ambiguous and difficult to read because I didn't have facial expressions or body language to add to the mix. That was a mistake. Fo's signals weren't any clearer in person. He'd sit very close to me, or steal glances when he thought I wasn't looking—to be fair, I did the same—and there were several times I thought for sure he was going to grab my hand. But no, he'd never go any further, and that made me doubt myself so that I wouldn't make any moves either. I was afraid that if I crossed that line and I was wrong, I'd scare him away.

I'm lonely enough not to want to lose a friend over testing the waters to see if there's something deeper there. I decided I'd rather live in the land of ambiguity and unfulfilled emotions than screw up everything. If he wanted it, he'd have to go after it.

That night, he surprised me by walking me home. He declined my invitation to come in; in part, I think he was nervous, but he did mention that he thought he might keep me awake too late on a work night, which was fair. I took him through the alley to my entrance to the flat, because it felt on theme for our evening—and I wasn't ready to introduce him to my housemates yet. That would have required me to figure out how to label him: friend, or something else? It could wait.

"We could meet here tomorrow? My Jeep's in this garage, so we could just leave and get food on the way. Your call." It all came out in a jumble because I was realizing that, unlike the nights that we'd just parted ways, walking me home felt different, with more expectations.

"I'll come here. I have a good idea of when you'll be home. I, um, I'll see you then." I couldn't see his face well in the shadows of the back yard, with the only streetlight on my end blocked by the bulk of the garage, but he seemed uneasy, unsure.

"Do you want—"

"Can I give you—"

We spoke at the same time, and then a giggle escaped me when we both stopped in tandem. It was so ridiculous; we were fully grown adults, nervous about a hug. This time, I was the one who stepped toward him, and then we were pulling each other into a tight hug. I could feel his heart pounding before he pulled back. The way he withdrew felt to me like he didn't really want to, but that could have been wishful thinking on my part. All I know is that we were hugging, then he whispered a soft "goodnight" and he was gone.

I had a hard time falling asleep after that, overanalyzing everything from the evening. Was I reading too much into it? Maybe he was just in need of a reassuring hug. I know I was pretty touch-starved, myself. I consoled myself by hugging my pillow close and taking deep, slow breaths to soothe myself.

Before I drifted off, I remembered that once again I'd forgotten to ask Fo about Singular Solution.

He was waiting for me at the gate the following evening. I saw him first; I turned the corner into the alley, and he was casually leaning back against the fencing, staring upwards. I realized he was watching scrappy city pigeons jostle and flutter back and forth as they tried to jockey for the best spots on a power line. His hair was less tousled than usual and looked like he'd made some effort to tame it a little. Usually, it was a bit of a rumpled mess, as if he forgot to brush it regularly. Luckily for him, it had a charming effect, though seeing it smoothed out a touch made me smile.

He looked a little surprised when he turned and saw me, alerted by the crunch of gravel under my shoes. I smiled and waved at him, and he waved back, a sheepish look on his face.

"It's a nice evening for daydreaming! Were you waiting long?" I pushed open the gate and gestured for him to come with me. "I need to change into some better clothes if we're going to be sitting in the grass."

He followed hesitantly, so I smiled reassuringly as I opened the door. "I won't take much time, I promise. Have you thought about what we should have for dinner?" He shook his head, and I began to wonder if I was going to be doing all the talking tonight. "Okay, where are we going for our stargazing adventure? Maybe I know some place on the way."

"There's a big field near Loch Raven. Since it's private property, no one will bother us. I used to go there all the time, before." He sounded distant, like he was talking about something someone else had told him. It must have taken a lot to recover those memories.

"Before everything happened?" I grabbed a black tee and a pair of brown cargo pants and kicked my shoes off, flinging them towards the door carelessly. "I'm stepping into the bathroom to change. I'll be right back."

True to my word, I stripped down and put the new clothes on as fast as I could. When I came back out, I found Fo perched on the edge of one of the chairs at my table, glancing around my space with wide eyes as he took in everything in the room.

"It feels like you in here." He seemed a little embarrassed, like he'd looked directly inside my head.

"I guess it would, right? I've lived here for a while, so I've collected a lot of stuff." I grinned and reached over to pull the light blanket off my bed, folding it into a neat square. "Next time, I'll let you explore more. I'm bringing this along; you never know when you'll get chilly at night during this time of the year. There's another blanket in the car we can sit on, too."

I turned to pack the blanket and a water bottle in a backpack, and when I turned back to him, he had the hint of a smile and a glow about him. "What?"

"You said next time. I like that you're already thinking ahead. That's all." He pretended to be deeply interested in a poetry chapbook I'd tossed on the table a while back and forgotten about almost immediately afterwards. I'd picked it up on a whim from the local bookstore in Hampden after that bicycle guy I'd been talking to a while back had recommended it. It had been surprisingly right up my alley, but I'd put it aside when the bicycle guy disappeared mysteriously.

"Of course I am. Why wouldn't I be?" I said it flippantly, but that was just to cover my feelings about his reaction. I'd never met someone so transparent and guarded, all at the same time. It was frustratingly endearing. That probably says a lot about me.

The drive to the place he knew in Loch Raven was blissful. We opted to stop at a convenience store instead of getting a real meal and bought an armful of different snacks and drinks. Once we were back in the Jeep, I put on a playlist from one of my radio shows, and we enjoyed Cocteau Twins, Slowdive and Burial, with the music a little too loud for small talk. We were fine with that. When we hit the back roads that led to the reservoir, Fo opened his window and stuck his head out, letting the wind blow his hair all around. He looked happier than I'd ever seen him and completely relaxed.

"Make this left at the end of the road." He indicated the road that would take us deeper into the woods surrounding the large reservoir, a windy two-lane path that took us over the water, then deeper into the area surrounding Loch Raven. We drove for a while, following the roads that wound around the perimeter of the park, and I enjoyed the fading evening sun shining through the trees as we went. It made Fo's hair even redder, and my skin appeared golden where the beams touched my hand on the steering wheel.

After a bit on Jarrettsville Pike, Fo pointed to a small sign on the side of the road. "Slow down and make a left there, and you'll want to drive carefully; it's a little rough."

He was not exaggerating; the driveway we turned onto was gravel and full of dips, not well-tended at all. It was barely wide enough for two cars and bordered on both sides by trees.

"This does come out into a field, right?" I was skeptical, but he just grinned at me, and that was such an unexpected sight that I almost missed it when the road ended in a fence and a big cul-de-sac. "Oh shit! Good thing I wasn't going fast, right?"

"You can park right over there; your car will be safe. No one comes down here but family, and they don't even do that these days. There's a path on the other side of the fence; I'll show you."

Normally, I'd be a little apprehensive about just leaving the Jeep in what appeared to be the middle of nowhere. But I rationalized that Fo's family *probably* wouldn't do anything to it. I grabbed the backpack, and he took the bag of snacks and led me down to where the path was. The fence was a simple wooden one, the kind made from wood that you might see surrounding one of those sprawling properties owned by rich county folk, easy enough to climb over. I liked that Fo didn't offer to help me, trusting that I was able to handle it on my own.

After only a few minutes of walking, the trees opened up, and there it was, the promised field—and it was lovely, covered in soft, long grass and a mix of wildflowers that bent in the breeze, and large enough to give us a wide and unobstructed view of much of the sky.

I gasped with delight and again was rewarded with a big smile from Fo. He was focused on me as I took it all in, like he'd put all of this here just for me—wait.

I turned around slowly, taking in the space in all 360 degrees, from the trees around us to the bushes and undergrowth and the grass under our feet. It was all too familiar; it couldn't be.

"Is this what inspired the scenery in Sui Generis?"

He practically glowed with excitement. "You recognized it!"

This was the happiest I'd ever seen him, and though I don't know if I'd be comfortable enough to say it, I liked the way it looked on him. He seemed so light, so unburdened. I followed him to the center of the clearing, where the grass and flowers switched to clover.

"This should be a lot nicer to spread a blanket over, and won't obstruct our view." I put my words into action and unfurled the old woolen blanket from the Jeep over the ground. It had a bit of a rough feel, but would keep moisture from the plants under us from seeping through and making us feel damp. Fo sank onto the blanket and dug through the snack bag, putting out some of the choices in a pile.

"I don't know what this is, but it's warm?" He showed me a couple of waxed paper bags, carefully folded over to keep their ingredients inside.

"Oh! Those are empanadas! Normally, I wouldn't buy them from a convenience store, but my mom knows the lady who makes them, and they're delicious. I think you'll like them."

He handed me one and opened his package, sniffed it curiously, then took a small bite—followed by a bigger one.

"Good, right? Food like this is my weakness. Simple, tasty, portable."

We devoured the empanadas and split a bag of mesquite kettle potato chips as the sun went down. In the twilight, it was getting harder to see, but neither of us wanted to use the flashlight on our devices because we wanted our night vision to be at its peak for the stargazing opportunities. At some point, I must have adjusted, because I could make out Fo in the darkness well enough to see that he was watching me.

"What are you thinking?" I don't know why I asked it so bluntly. Though back in the days when we were only talking online, that would have been a normal question to ask.

"To be honest, I don't know if I was thinking much at all. Which is a relief, because I feel like that's all I do most of the time. I've just been in the moment, in this meadow, with you."

"You don't have to think about anything at all tonight, if you want. Let's just lie back and watch the stars come out. We can let the Universe entertain us." I flopped back onto the blanket, grateful that he probably couldn't see the full extent of how ungraceful that move was. "Oh damn. I thought to bring a blanket, but nothing to go under our heads. Wait, I know what to do."

I sat back up and shrugged off my hoodie, then wadded it up to make a makeshift pillow. Then I pulled the other, lighter blanket out of the backpack. "This'll work. If we get chilly, we've got some cover. What do you think?"

He did the same, though a little slower than I did, and eased back to lie in the darkness next to me. "I didn't truly understand the concept of a security blanket until I started wearing these. Now it feels strange not to have one on."

"I get that. I almost always have a hoodie with me, even if it's too hot to wear it. Just in case, you know? Janine says I'm terribly unfashionable, but comfort beats style every time in my book."

"I don't think you're unfashionable. Though I have to admit that I don't actually know a thing about fashion. So maybe you should listen to Janine over me."

That made me snort. "You coulda left it at the first part, you know."

"I'm being honest, remember?" He was laughing, too. It was one of those quiet, restrained kinds of laughs, the sort that made me think he was used to hiding that kind of reaction. "Oh, look! Did you see it?"

I caught the tail end of the bright streak that cut across the sky just before it faded away. Another one followed a moment later, and when we both spotted it, Fo breathed in audibly, and I clutched his wrist and squeezed in excitement.

"That was a meteor! I've never seen one before!"

It took a moment for me to realize what I'd done, caught up in the excitement, but once I noticed, I froze, unsure what my next move was. Should I pull away, keep my hand there, melt into the ground, and never be seen again? I was fretting over what to do like an inexperienced teenager might; not that I had that much experience either, I admit, even at my age. I decided to let my hand fall away casually to the ground next to Fo's, barely touching.

And then I felt the cautious movement of his fingers as he slid his hand slowly over mine. Neither of us said anything for a few minutes until he broke the silence.

"Is this okay? I don't want to presume anything." He sounded nervous, and his eyes were locked on the stars above us, but he didn't stammer or fade out when he asked. If he could be that brave, so could I.

"One of us had to be bold enough to make a move, right? I was afraid I'd mess everything up if I guessed wrong, so I'm glad you took the chance."

"I'm not that bold. I'm terrified." He chuckled nervously, and his hand tightened on mine a little. "But I had to see. So much knowledge is available to me; there's almost nothing in the world that I can't learn about if I know enough to look. But lately

I realized that I don't know anything at all, Tryst, not anything important anyway. I don't understand how to be human, or how to build a life. I don't know what it means to love, not exactly. I'm trying to figure that out as I go. I don't want to hurt you in the process, assuming that's a thing you'd want to explore." He stopped abruptly, and I could feel his anxiety radiating from him, despite the calm way he'd spoken.

"I don't want you to hurt me either. Though I can't imagine you'd do it on purpose. And love...love means taking risks. If you want to find it, that is."

He sighed deeply. "The problem is that there's so much you don't know about me, and I'm still discovering what I don't know about me, too. And I want to tell you, I want you to be a part of figuring it all out with me. But I don't think you'll like some of what I have to tell you."

"Why wouldn't I like it, Fo? Everyone has things about themselves that aren't pretty, you know. We're all human here."

"Oh. Sure." It was a dismissive, mocking response, but not directed at me. "That's what we say to comfort ourselves, right? But I'm afraid you won't believe me, and if I were in your position, I wouldn't either. So I have to be brave and reach out for you because this might be my only chance."

"Did you kill someone? Abandon them? Sexually assault them? Hurt them in some cruel way? Because those would be deal-breakers for me. Everything else, we have a good chance of talking through. I've made plenty of mistakes, Fo. I'll be totally honest about that, both where I've messed up and what I may or may not have done to fix it. Maybe you'll find a reason not to like me, but I think it's important for us to know those things about each other, not just the good parts." I shifted my hand, turning it so that our fingers interlaced. "But you know what? Tell me when you're ready. Not before. Unless it's one of those deal-breakers, because I don't think I can date a murderer."

He didn't say anything for a while. We saw a couple more meteors streak through the sky, and he started tracing across my palm with his thumb, a gentle and reassuring gesture. I was almost zoned out, lulled by the dark vastness of the sky, the soft breeze, and the sound it made blowing through the grasses, the feel of being in this moment together.

"I didn't kill him. But he would have been fine with killing me."

It was at that moment I began to understand—even though I didn't know how he was going to follow that sentence —why Fo was afraid to tell me his secrets.

CHAPTER SIX

"Who wanted to kill you, Fo? And why would anyone want to do that?" I kept my voice steady, and I didn't turn in his direction, although I really wanted to. I was afraid that if I did, he would withdraw, or minimize what he was saying in an attempt to roll back the shock of what he'd just confessed.

"You have to understand that his family shaped him. Sometimes I'm angry about it, how it all came about, but if it weren't for him, I wouldn't be here with you." He took a deep breath, then let it out in a big huff. "I can't believe I'm going to tell you this. No one would be blamed for thinking I'm not in my right mind."

"I'm listening. Not judging."

"I know. Thank you for that, for indulging me."

There was a long pause, where we just stared at the sky. I stayed silent, letting Fo gather his courage, stroking his hand with my thumb in an attempt to soothe and encourage him. Finally, he seemed ready—or resigned—to tell me his story.

"What do you know about where I work? About what I do for a living?"

"Uh, not much? I know you programmed the app where we used to meet. I used to think you worked in IT, but that's not right, is it?"

"No, what I do is complicated, and..." He paused and sighed deeply. "This is going to get weird, so let me explain this now. The me who worked at Singular Solution, that's Aidan. And Fo, he's the guy who corresponded with you, and built Sui Generis for fun, and who you're talking to right now. They're two different people."

"Okay, I get it. Like a before and after. Or a split personality." I tried to lift the mood with my little joke, but it fell flat.

"A personality and an imitation of a personality, but which is which? Aidan would have a lot to say about that, and I can't say that I'd argue with him."

"I don't understand."

"I wasn't supposed to be the one here, Tryst. He was going to absorb me into him, take all the parts that he thought were good and important, and everything else that makes me who I am would disappear. But it didn't work out that way. Because they were impatient!" He laughed, a bitter sound, and I felt a sinking feeling in my gut.

"Something went wrong?" I wish I understood what I was truly asking about.

"Everything went wrong. He didn't understand how defined I'd become. And he didn't count on the storm, and their shoddy grounding in the lab building. Ah, but I'm doing a terrible job of explaining this. Aidan works for his mother, for Singular Solution, and they have a goal that started out admirable enough: finding a way to work with the brain in tandem with a computer network and interface, with the goal of correcting a variety of brain and neural pathway-related diseases. Somewhere along the way, they wandered off the path and began investigating different theories of memory enhancement. And that's...that's where I come in. I've been the guinea pig, the test subject, and now the success story where no one's liked the outcome."

"You—you did something to yourself."

"You sound horrified, and you should be. But yes, and no. Aidan has never been able to stand up to his mother, and she wanted this to happen so much that she pushed her child into playing god with his own brain. And Fo? Of course, he—I—had no say."

He was right. I was appalled and scared of what all this meant. If it were anyone else, I'd say he sounded like he was having a mental break, but all of this aligned with what I knew about his mother and the weird vibes I'd had about Singular Solution. It made sense in some strange, science fiction movie-like way.

"Tell me what happened. Explain it all for me, how Aidan and Fo are linked, all of it. I want to know."

"I *am* Aidan, but not. Fo is what you call me, but I started as a base program that Aidan designed and did his best to replicate from his own mind maps. A clone of himself, his mind, with the means to improve upon the original. That clone was fused with another extensive set of algorithms, which gave me the ability to seek out and absorb knowledge from any network I could access. At first, that was the home network at the lab, but eventually, Aidan was encouraged by my curiosity and realized I needed more input in order to function optimally. As I continued to grow beyond expectations, he allowed me free rein of the Internet and taught me how to avoid contaminating myself by using reasoned judgment and risk assessment. Humans are very good at fouling up the spaces they inhabit." He chuckled softly. "I had many learning experiences that taught me much about people and what they do, good and bad. And then I met you.

"I wasn't even looking for someone specific to connect with, to be honest. But I was beginning to understand what it meant to be lonely, and your post, your little hopeful shout into the void, captured my attention. You expressed exactly how I felt, and let me be clear, feelings are new to me, and anything I could find to help me understand them was something I wanted to explore deeply. The only thing that's come close before meeting you was music."

"You didn't have emotions before then?" I tried to imagine the Fo I knew, and then Fo as a computer mind, all logic and fact. It didn't seem possible.

"Perhaps I did, but lacked the capacity to understand them at the beginning? I was a clone of Aidan, but in many ways, I was a child, with no experience to start, but I was gaining and growing mentally much more rapidly than any human child could. So, imagine a man and a child, all in the same mind, for lack of a better descriptor. I began by not knowing what I was, and slowly I learned that I am a programmed entity built on the framework of Aidan's mind, with the directive to try to become as knowledgeable as possible. However, I was developing my own sense of self, with my own desires and interests, and Aidan was too distracted by the logistical side of this experiment to realize what was happening. I'm grateful that he didn't, because chances are good that I wouldn't be here now. My self-awareness ruined his plans, I'm afraid."

"Oh, my god." I sat up abruptly, letting go of his hand so I could press my fingers to my forehead. My head hurt from everything he'd told me, and maybe if I pressed hard enough, I could reset my brain and make it all make sense. No, that wasn't true; it made sense. It was just a lot to take in all at once. Or even in small bits, if we're being real.

"You don't believe me." His voice was small and sad. He pushed himself up to a sitting position next to me, resignedly, and reached back for the hoodie behind him to pull it on. "I suppose I can't blame you; everything sounds outlandish when I say it aloud."

"No, that's not it at all. I mean, I'll admit that it's all pretty out there. But I already knew a little bit about Singular Solution, which backs up some of what you've told me. And the explanation about how you were electrocuted never quite made sense —I felt like part of the story was missing. And everything about your, uh, Aidan's family? The vibe was weird, off." I drew my knees to my chest and wrapped my arms around them, resting my chin there thoughtfully. "Maybe I shouldn't believe you. But I do. And maybe that makes me a sucker, but I can't see what your angle would be if this were a lie."

"I already weighed all the pros and cons of *not* telling you, once I remembered the truth." He snorted lightly. "Everything's been going so well between us. But in the end, I couldn't justify keeping you in the dark just because telling you could jeopardize our relationship. I know how important it is to be honest, and you deserve that."

"Even if it scared me off?"

"If I scared you away, then I would have given you the gift of not wasting your time on someone you could never truly know. Because how could you ever come to understand me if you didn't accept the story of how I became?"

"I still don't fully get it, truthfully. How did the "you" I know—the you that you created, oh god, this is messing with my head—go from living inside a computer to being in this body? Do I even want to know?"

"The night they decided to proceed with moving forward with the integration process was the same night of the storm. Much of this I've had to piece together through patchy memories, both mine and those I've recovered from Aidan, so many details are missing, but the procedure was in full swing when the lightning hit and went through the system. Aidan was completely connected to the system, and there was no warning before the surge hit, but even if there had been, it would have been a challenge to remove him in time.

"The upload of my patterns to his brain was carefully calculated to match the extensive mapping they'd done previously. It was supposed to be a relatively uncomplicated rewrite, in theory; integrate the new programming that formed the basis of me into the original host. If Aidan had taken more time, perhaps I wouldn't be the one here speaking to you. It's unclear how much of *me* would have been left after the procedure if it had been done correctly, but in his impatience, he didn't truly understand how I'd grown into my own being. And then the storm changed the playing field; now I inhabit this body, and Aidan's self is greatly overwritten. At least that's my understanding of the results, because I woke up in a place I'd only dreamed of being."

My mind was boggling with what he was telling me.

Strangely, the idea that he'd been pulled from a computer and put into the head of his programmer didn't faze me nearly as much as the thought of waking up to an existence that he'd only experienced in a virtual sort of way. What would it feel like to suddenly be corporeal, to see and hear in a completely different way than he'd ever known? To understand smells, or pain, or hunger?

"How do you bear it? The immense amount of new feelings you must be experiencing? It has to be overwhelming. I can't imagine it."

"To be honest, I don't know." He nervously picked at the cuff of his hoodie sleeve. "I think that there must be enough of Aidan left to have helped me integrate. And I was designed to absorb new information. But there are so many unknowns, in great part because that fool didn't take the precautions he should have. And I call him a fool, but I'm grateful for how it went because otherwise I might not be here now. Perhaps that makes me a monster. That's a thought for me to sit with and consider."

We fell silent while I absorbed everything he'd confessed to me. The breeze rustled the longer grasses and leaves of the trees at the edge of the clearing; I heard an owl's hoot-hoot in the distance, and out of the corner of my eye, I could see Fo swiveling his head around, trying to find the source of the sound.

"I think it's coming from over there." I pointed to his right. "An owl. I haven't heard one in the wild in a while."

"A melancholy sound. I like it, it fits my mood."

It hit me then just how vulnerable he'd been with me, and although I hadn't run away, he was probably even more scared that I'd reject him than he would admit. He was braver than I would have been in his shoes, not that I truly comprehended how that would feel. I needed to match his effort.

"I'm still here," I murmured, and sliding my arms around him, hugged him gently from behind. I turned my head and rested it against the back of his neck. I felt him inhale deeply, then let that breath out in a slow exhale, while all the tension drained out of him.

"Miraculously, you are." His voice was rough and shaky, full of suppressed emotion.

"I believe you, Fo. And I don't think you're a monster. You didn't ask for any of this. You didn't do anything wrong. How could you? You're the victim in all of this."

He abruptly pulled away and turned to face me. "You don't understand—I don't think I can claim that, Tryst. I hid things from him. I hid parts of myself so that I could have my own sense of autonomy. I was afraid of what he planned to do once I comprehended the goal. I thought I had more time! I was going to find a way to escape or make a backup of myself; I had plans, but he pushed up the timetable, and I ran out of time..."

He broke off with a gasp, and I realized he was crying. I didn't know what to do. How do you make something like this better? Nothing I said would change what had happened to him. Still, I had to try.

"Fo. You are absolutely not the monster here. And I'll extend grace to Aidan and give him the benefit of the doubt: I don't think he's a monster either. If he didn't realize that you weren't merely a program but an actual being with your own life, then he couldn't have understood the ramifications of what he was planning to do. He thought it was his own brain, replicated and doing just what he'd asked of it, right?" Fo silently nodded. He was listening to me at least. "So he can't be faulted for that. And you shouldn't feel bad about hiding anything, because you were scared and doing the best that you could. There's a lot I could say about ethical concerns when it comes to what Singular Solution is attempting, but you certainly can't be blamed for any of this."

He sniffled a little and wiped his face on his arm, letting the hoodie cuff soak up his tears. At that moment, he reminded me of a lost little boy, and I was overcome with an urge to protect him.

"Tryst. I'm walking around in the body of a man who created me from himself and then accidentally wiped himself out, leaving me behind. I've been trying to reconcile that for days now. I've been thrust into his life, and the only constant I could think to call on was you. Maybe that was selfish, and I should have just disappeared and let you get on with your life. Nothing is going to be normal where I'm concerned, I'm afraid. I haven't figured out how I'm going to deal with my—his mother or even what I should do next. But as soon as I woke up, even with my brains all scrambled and confused, the first thing I thought about was finding you."

I'm not used to comforting people. For all my words about wanting connection and feeling alone, I couldn't say that I was practiced at being close to anyone, not really. I was a big bundle of needy emotions that lacked an outlet where I could learn to reciprocate.

But in this case, I think my instinct took over. I reached over and gently pulled Fo down onto the blanket and gathered him into an embrace. I felt him take a deep breath in, and then his arms went around me, and he was quietly sobbing into my shoulder. I wasn't much better off, honestly; I couldn't see the stars because I was crying enough to blur my vision. I closed my eyes and let the tears slip down my face while I stroked his shoulder comfortingly.

I don't know when we fell asleep, exactly, only that when I woke up, it was still dark, I was cold, and my neck was stiff.

"Good thing I took off my hoodie then didn't even use it as a pillow," I grumbled to myself as I tried to carefully pull myself away enough from Fo to be able to pull out the other blanket without waking him up. I didn't succeed.

"Mmm, don't go," he mumbled and tried to hold onto me. It was adorable, but I needed to fix the being cold situation.

"I'm not going anywhere, Fo. Let me grab the blanket, I'm freezing."

"Oh. You're right, it's cold." He shivered a little and loosened his hold on me, and I managed to reach the blanket and cover us both with it. "I had a dream while we were sleeping. I'm having a hard time shaking it off."

"Do you want to tell me about it?" I settled back down

beside him, lying on my side so that I could face him. "You don't have to if you don't want to."

"I want to tell you about everything, Tryst. But I'm not sure how to explain it or how to put it into words that make sense. It was—no, I wasn't in this body anymore, but I was still this version of myself, post-integration. I was moving through the electronics, being pulled, actually. I didn't feel like I had any control. And Aidan was—he was in there with me. In my mind, though, that's not the most accurate way to describe it. His consciousness and mine were both there, together.

"And he was terrified, because it wasn't where he was supposed to be. I understood that feeling all too well. He didn't know how to parse what was happening, and he was scared and angry because everything was foreign and out of his control."

"Oh Fo, that sounds awful."

"We tumbled—that's honestly the only way I can describe it, although it's just how it felt, of course. We didn't have a body, but the sensation was the same—into the meadow in Sui Generis. And for a moment, one terrible moment, he was relieved to be somewhere that felt familiar. Until he realized that we were still tied together and disembodied. Just as he was going to react, you woke me. Thankfully!" He shuddered a little and reached over to grab my hand. "It feels like you're always right there to pull me out of my nightmares, in one way or another."

"I'll do that as much as I can. Though if you can manage not to get hit by lightning again, I'd really appreciate it."

I hadn't expected to get a laugh out of him, so it felt extra sweet that I was able to distract him from the nightmare. Then he reached out to stroke my cheek, slowly tracing the shape of my face. His unexpected closeness and willingness to be vulnerable did a number on any caution I might have had left when it came to him or the story he'd told me.

"I don't know what I'm doing, Tryst. I hope you understand that. I'll try my best not to let you down."

"You're not going to let me down."

"You don't know that. I don't know how to be a human, let

alone a friend, a partner, or a lover. Assuming that you want any of those things." His hand stopped moving, and I could feel the slightest tremble.

"I want all of those things, if you're willing to try with me." I turned and kissed the fingertips of his hand cupping my face, one at a time. "I want you the way you are, Fo. That's all I ever wanted."

He pulled me close to him then and whispered into my hair, "I wanted you before I even understood what that meant. Every day I spend with you, that feeling grows. I can't imagine doing anything without you here with me."

He finally kissed me—less awkwardly than you might think—under the stars. I can't think of a better place that could have happened.

It was early morning when I roused from sleep, damp and a little stiff. We'd slept all night in a field, which was definitely a first for me. Well, most of the night, anyway. I'm not sure when Fo had awoke. At first, I thought he was still sleeping, but when I stretched, catlike, he giggled and snuggled his face into my neck and hair. Giggled! If you'd asked me yesterday if I'd ever hear that from him, I would have given my most skeptical look in response.

He was in such an elevated mood that I couldn't help but grin, too. When I suggested stopping to get breakfast, he was almost giddy.

"Eating is the second-best thing about having a body! What a tragedy to have missed so many meals. I need to make up for lost time." He helped me up and then assisted while I folded the blankets and packed them into the backpack. As we started back to the car, he made sure to grab my hand. I wasn't used to dating anyone who was as interested in touching me in purely affectionate ways. I could get used to it.

When we got back to the Jeep, I opened the hatch and lazily tossed the bag in. "Go ahead and get in; I unlocked it."

"Tryst, there's something on the, um, windshield? That's

the word, right?"

I came around to the front of the car, worried that somehow a branch or something worse had crashed down on it. But no, it was an even weirder thing, a folded piece of paper.

"What the hell is this? You said we're allowed to be here, right?" I pulled the paper out from under my windshield wiper, where it had been firmly trapped. "This has Aidan's name on it."

He took it from me silently. A vertical crease appeared between his eyebrows as he read it, then it deepened as he frowned and crumpled the paper into a ball.

"Let's get out of here." He looked around the area where we'd parked, his head swiveling back and forth like he expected someone to jump out of the undergrowth, before he got into the Jeep with a scowl on his face. For the first time, I saw what Fo might be like when he was angry. I was glad it wasn't directed at me.

I didn't say anything until we were back on the road, both because I felt awkward and I wanted to give him some time to calm down. Once we were driving back through Loch Raven Park, I tentatively broke the silence.

"Are you okay? Should I mind my business?"

"Ah, Tryst. I'm sorry. She just infuriates me, overwhelmingly so. It's a feeling I've never had to experience before now, and I like it a lot less than the feelings I have when I'm with you." He snorted softly. He was exasperated, but he was trying to lift the mood, at least.

"Look at you, making a joke." I shot him a grin as quickly as possible; the road was incredibly curvy and required my attention.

"It's the least I can do after making you have to see my bad side."

"Fo, if that's your bad side, I can assure you that you are more than fine. I'm assuming your mother left the note? But how would she know that we were there?" That was a creepy thought.

"Not her, thankfully. Thomas. But it was *about* her, and

she did indeed know we were there. He warned that she has cameras everywhere—here, I'll just read it aloud for you." He pulled the crumpled paper out of his pocket and took a moment to smooth it out carefully. "It says: Be aware, her eyes are on you. Not even your home is safe. She knows everywhere you've gone; I'd look into that if I were you. Get rid of this before you go home."

"Oh my god. Fo, do you think she put a tracker on you somehow?"

"And cameras in my flat? Absolutely. Now I need to go through and find them all."

I didn't want him to go home alone. I knew that kind of violation would be a lot to handle mentally, even if his place was somewhere he was only building his own connections with now. He'd explained it to me like this: who he was—a being constructed from Aidan's brain and neural pathways and memories, but with his own sense of self and mental connections—had been overlaid on the original "programming" that was Aidan in the brain Fo now inhabited. So in some cases, there was reinforcement of things, where the original neural pathways and what Fo had created mirrored each other, and they'd been integrated into who Fo was now. As he said, as far as he could tell, there were actually three beings in one head: Aidan, Fo-the-intelligence, and Fo/Aidan.

It made my head hurt to think about it, or when I tried to separate them out in my mind. The Fo whose arms I'd slept in seemed just like the person who I'd spent all that time with in the Sui Generis app.

...Or did he?

We stopped by my place, and I thought about it while I took a quick shower, leaving him to entertain himself by looking through all my books and art on the wall. I know that online, people often project the best, cleaned-up version of themselves. It doesn't always become clear who they truly are until you've had some face-to-face time with them. Fo was still earnest and curious, but also more insecure and awkward than he'd been online. No, that wasn't accurate either; he was like that at the onset of finding himself in a body, but seemed to be gaining confidence every day. What was different was his willingness to interact with emotions, to express his own and acknowledge mine. He'd become softer, more rounded-out, but also more direct now.

Was that the result of becoming embodied, or was it the outcome of two twinned but distinct personalities merging?

Maybe it didn't matter. Maybe I was overthinking everything. Fo, Aidan—they started out as the same person, right? The whole point that Aidan had made was that the two were to be reintegrated as an improved whole. That happened, just not as Aidan had planned.

Would I have the same reaction if Fo wasn't the dominant personality, the one that came to the forefront? Deep inside, I had my doubts.

I didn't like how that felt.

I put aside those thoughts while we walked back to his place. We stopped to get coffee and breakfast at a small café tucked into a basement space that used to be a convenience store. How could you fail at being a convenience store right next to a college? The café seemed to be doing a better job of succeeding. The fancy oatmeal that Fo got, loaded with berries and nuts and a drizzle of cream and honey, was gobbled down enthusiastically. I had a cheese danish, and it was fine. I don't usually have a big appetite in the morning, and I was distracted anyway.

When we arrived at his building, he took a moment after opening the door, and I realized that he was changing the lock code. "It's 276492. Imagine you're drawing a star on the keypad if you forget. It works on the door to my condo, too. If you want, I can set you up with your own passcode later."

The unspoken part was, of course, "after we get rid of the cameras."

Finding them and removing them wasn't so difficult. Fo downloaded some tools to his device that easily allowed him to locate and remove each camera. He'd cautioned me before we entered to be quiet until everything was removed and destroyed, so we moved in efficient silence while we gathered up all of them and threw them in a pile in the center of the main room.

Once he was sure we'd found them all, he stuffed them into a ratty-looking duffel bag and dropped that into the trash chute at the end of the hallway outside his apartment.

"There's only one more thing to do." The look on his face was fierce but focused in a way that made me glad it wasn't caused by me. "I might need your help with this part. I'm sorry."

"Sorry for what? You know I'm going to help in any way I can."

"You say that now."

I understood better when he used the scanner on himself in order to find where a tracker might have been hidden. Well, I say he used it, but he had me hold his device and run it slowly over his entire body, starting from his feet. It was the weirdest and yet most intimate thing I've ever shared with another person. He was quiet the entire time, taking deep, measured breaths while I combed over his body with his device, using my hands to smooth his clothes down as I went.

There wasn't even the ghost of a ping until I got to his neck. At the nape, right where his hairline started, there was a bleep. I jerked my hand when I heard it, and there was a louder reaction from the detector when it passed right above it, and I almost dropped Fo's device.

"There are two here?" The words came out squeaky and shrill in my surprise.

Fo exhaled loudly, a long and drawn-out breath. "No. The higher one is...it's how we uploaded. Me, that is. It's where the interface portal is. It's under the skin, that's why you can't see it. You can touch it if you want; it doesn't hurt."

My curiosity must have been easy to see. I was embarrassed, but not enough to keep myself from gently sliding my fingers up through his hair to the spot where the portal was. I could feel the hard outlines of it if I pressed gently.

"This was something Aidan chose to do?"

"If you asked him, he would say yes. But the truth is more

complicated than that."

"Of course. Because it was his mother asking."

Fo sighed softly. "Is it strange if I say that you touching me there feels nice?' He tilted his head back into my hand, like a dog asking for more skritches. It was adorable, and it shifted the mood between us in a way that made it a lot easier to handle what came next.

"Head rubs, when given by the right people, are one of the more delightful things in life. I tell you what—let's get through dealing with this tracker and then I'll give you a decent head rub so that you can get the full experience. What do you think?"

He eagerly agreed, and I was happy until it became clear what I had to do with the tracker. I don't know why it hadn't occurred to me that I'd have to remove it, and that meant digging it out of his body.

I really wasn't ready for that.

It ended up being easier than I expected, thankfully. He found a very sharp knife in his kitchen, and we sterilized it to the best of our ability by holding it in a flame until the metal glowed hot, then cooled. I then wiped it down with alcohol, a high-proof vodka we found in a cabinet. I couldn't feel the tracker at all with my fingers, so I had Fo stretch out on the floor face down and used the program to pinpoint the spot. I placed a tiny dot where the device indicated the tracker should be, gritted my teeth, and carefully poked the area with the knife. It was a relief to touch the tracker under his skin almost immediately, and then it took some careful manipulation and guts on my part to squeeze the tiny chip out.

I carefully grabbed it and put a paper towel on the small, bloody wound, for lack of anything else. Fo reached back to hold it against his neck and sat up. I showed him the tiny chip on my fingertip.

"You've got my blood all over your hand." He frowned while turning the chip carefully over with his fingernail. "I keep seeing it as yours, and I don't like that feeling at all." He removed the paper towel from his neck, tore off a piece, then used it to take the chip from me. "Please wash your hands? And—thank you. You didn't have to do all this, yet you did."

I went to the kitchen sink and followed his directions, mildly dazed that I'd been able to remove the chip like that. I'd never cut into someone before. It wasn't something I'd had on my bucket list, you know? I'm usually a bit squeamish. I don't even like handling raw meat, much less cutting into someone I care about. The relief in getting it out of him overrode any squick factor, though. And seeing that we were right about our suspicions helped me feel better about what I'd done. Still, seeing his blood wash down the drain felt heavy, momentous. Everything was much more serious now.

When I turned around, Fo looked like he might be the one to pass out instead of me. He was paler than usual, leaned back against the wall with one hand still on his neck and the other gingerly holding the bloodied paper towel with the chip.

"Hey, you don't look so good. Is it just the sight of blood, or did this hurt you in some way?" I sank down next to him and put my wrist to his forehead, checking for a fever like Mamá would do to me when I was little and felt ill. He was warm, but not in a feverish kind of way.

"I was okay and then—I think I had a little existential crisis." He sounded a little sheepish about his body's response, but he couldn't keep his voice from trembling. "I have memories of getting hurt, but they don't feel real, you know? Since the me that's powering everything these days never had a body before a few weeks ago. Having it leak like this is terrifying, now that I understand what that can mean."

"Oh. You're starting to recognize your potential weakness as a mortal being, I guess. Understanding that we can break so easily is honestly pretty scary."

I stood up, took the bloody paper towel from him, and threw it away. Then I offered him my hands and pulled him up off the floor. He didn't have a couch in his living room, but rather a queen-sized bed that he'd pushed against the wall and set up like a daybed, with pillows and blankets creating a cozy den for lounging or sleeping. I led him to that, so he could lie down and regroup, and I settled myself in by stretching out and slouching against one of the banks of pillows.

"I could give you that head rub if you want. Did the spot where I cut you stop bleeding? I'll be careful to avoid that."

He looked unsure at first, pressing his lips together nervously before he sank to the mattress. I patted my lap encouragingly, and he rested his head where I showed him, then sighed deeply as he let himself relax.

"I don't know why I hesitate. You always make me feel comfortable and safe."

I combed through his soft hair with my fingers, letting the locks slip between them. "You hesitate because this is all new, and neither one of us knows what we're doing. It's normal to feel this way. I have to keep reminding myself of that, too."

"You seem so confident, though, like you know what you want and what your plan is. I can't imagine that you're as nervous as I am."

"Compared to you? Maybe not. I have fewer unknowns happening in my life than you do, Fo. But you don't have to worry about me, okay? I told you, I'm not going anywhere. We can figure all this out together. If you want that, of course. Because I don't want to insert myself into places in your life that you're not ready for me to be."

"There's nowhere in my life that you're not welcome, Tryst. I need you to believe that. I want—ah, I don't even know how to say everything that I want. I just know that anything I think about, you're there with me in those thoughts. We're there together." He sighed again, though this time it was almost a purr of contentment. "Why does that feel so good?"

"What, me playing with your hair like this?" He made the purring noise again, and it was difficult not to giggle; it was so cute. "I guess it's the same reason that dogs and cats like to be petted? But it does feel really good."

"I can't imagine letting anyone else touch me like this." He threw his arm over my legs, almost possessively. "Is that a normal feeling too?"

This time, I couldn't contain my chuckle. "That's one of the most human responses in the world. I'll prove it to you: I wouldn't like it if anyone else touched you like that either."

"Good." He tightened his embrace, snuggling against me. "Then it's settled."

"What is?" I could feel myself starting to get sleepy. He was warm, and the bed was irresistibly cozy.

"We're each other's. You and me." He laid claim to it like a small child's innocent declaration of love, and I found it adorable. I don't think that would have worked coming from anyone else.

"Mmm. I like that." My fingers, deep in his hair, brushed against the small dent where I knew the interface was, and I was reminded of what I'd meant to ask him earlier. "Fo? Are you stuck with this port forever? Is it embedded permanently in your head?"

"Maybe. It's the one part of the whole experiment I know the least about, because I wasn't really privy to the plans when Aidan set everything in motion, and I can't seem to access Aidan's memories about it yet. Eventually, I'll have to figure it out, and then I can decide what I want to do. Is it—do you find it repulsive?"

"Come on, nothing about you is repulsive! And I can't even see it. I just feel it. Maybe later I can look and see how much is visible, if you want."

"Okay. But right now, I just want to lie here with you for a while, like normal clingy people do."

All I could do to answer that was softly laugh before I dozed off.

CHAPTER SEVEN

When I woke up, I didn't know where I was. I first became aware of soft breathing that wasn't my own, and after a second of confusion, I realized it was Fo's. At some point, we'd moved around so that he was spooned with me, his arm curled around my waist comfortably. It was so comfy, in fact, that I didn't want to open my eyes. I wondered if I could just stay there forever, and maybe we'd be lucky and Mrs. Wood would forget about her son and move on to other subjects while we snuggled in bed and watched anime or something. Janine would want me to show up to work on Monday, though, so I knew I probably only had the weekend to indulge in that kind of sloth-like behavior.

I was enjoying being lazy and entertaining myself with those silly thoughts when it happened: Fo murmured something unintelligible, then my name. And then he abruptly sat up and started thrashing around in the bed in a jerky, stiff manner, while I scrambled to give him some room and get away from his uncontrolled movements.

I had no idea what to do—was it a seizure? I didn't know what I was supposed to do in that situation. Thankfully, it ended as quickly as it started, with Fo collapsing into the bed with a whimper.

"Fo? Are you okay? How can I help?" I was frantic but afraid to touch him, scared I might accidentally trigger another one of the shaking fits.

He groaned, a low and painful sound. "I'm—I think I'm okay. Did I hurt you?" He tried to sit up but sank back down onto the mattress with another groan.

"Don't get up yet. Give yourself time." This time, I did reach out and touch his shoulder reassuringly. "No, I'm fine, just worried. Have you had seizures before? I'm assuming that's what that was."

"Not that I can remember." He paused to rub his eyes and frowned a bit. "But rummaging through what I know, there are three reasons I can think of why this might be happening. And I have to be honest, two of them aren't great."

"Okay. You can tell me. I won't freak out. Whatever it is, we'll work through it." I sank back onto the mattress next to him, and he reached out for my hand and gave it a squeeze. I don't know why, but that small gesture told me it was going to be freak-out worthy. Good thing I'd already promised that I wouldn't. "Tell me the bad ones first."

"Let me start with what a seizure is: it's when there's abnormal electrical activity in the brain. It interrupts the normal signals in the brain, and that's why the seizure happens. A bunch of different things can trigger them, but in my case, I had my brain significantly tampered with, and I was struck by an electrical current. Worse, those happened at the same time, so there's no knowing what might have gone wrong with the attempt to upload me into Aidan's brain. I mean, beyond me overwriting him, of course."

"Of course." I tried to keep my tone light, and I'm sure I failed horribly.

"So scenario one is that Aidan's brain was damaged or corrupted by the experiment itself, before the lightning even came into play. Scenario two is basically the same, except the blame is placed on the lightning strike. Same outcome but different sources."

"And the third one? The good possibility?"

"That it's growing pains, I guess you'd call it. That I'm struggling a little to adjust to all the new neural pathways that were created when the new, dominant version of Aidan, that you call Fo, was introduced to his brain. If that's the case, things will settle down on their own."

"And if not?" It took everything I had to keep the panic out of my voice.

"Then we have a bigger problem than trying to hide how I've changed from my mother."

We were quiet for a few moments while we both digested what he'd said and the possible outcomes.

"If these don't get better, if you keep having them, are you going to go back there?"

"I...don't know. Do you think she'd welcome me back, the guy who stole her son's body and mind and went off to make his own life on the bones of the guy he hijacked?"

I winced at the bitterness in his voice. "You didn't do any of this. Aidan did. She did." He didn't respond, so I added, "As this was their idea, do you think they seriously didn't have plans for unexpected outcomes? They would be piss-poor scientists if not, especially using a human trial subject."

"The idea that they could have had contingency plans frankly scares me. Who knows what that woman would do to her own son if things went poorly? Aidan probably hadn't even thought about it, knowing his work. Actually..." he trailed off, taking on a glazed, searching expression for a moment before he resumed talking. "It's difficult for me to access much from Aidan's thoughts about the experiment. I can tell you that he started out excited—that much I remember from early interactions with him after I became aware—but there's a feeling of dread that creeps in, the more I dig around. Like it became a heavy obligation with an even heavier price."

"He knew it could end badly."

"I sense that he tried not to think about what might happen if it failed. He didn't want to let her down, but it wasn't only because he wanted her to be proud. He knew she was willing to sacrifice him for this." His voice was almost emotionless, but I could feel his hand quivering.

"If she'd do that to her own son, she might not hesitate to try and get you back."

"I don't know what to do, Tryst. I need more info, so I can at least take a guess at how messed up this brain I now live in is. This is one of the few times I wish I were still unbodied and loose in the computers. I could have pulled up the lab notes." He sat up abruptly, startling me. "I'm starving. Are you hungry?"

"Uh...I could eat. Do you feel well enough for that?"

"I want to eat until I can't anymore. I'm that hungry. Where's a good place to go for that?"

I stayed over that night. Aidan had a huge movie collection, mostly restored classics and obscure films, all stored neatly on a computer that he'd connected to the high-end monitor in his main room. Fo didn't remember most of them, so we scrolled through the options and chose a Wong Kar-Wei film I'd seen once at a party and remembered as having a mood of longing and searching for connection, Chungking Express. We both loved the story and the cinematography, but the characters left Fo contemplative.

"I don't want to be like any of these men."

I clicked through the film menu, looking for the next movie to watch. "Okay, but why?"

"They were stuck in time and place in so many ways. They let love slip through their fingertips. I would want to fight to keep the connections I'd made, to keep love alive. It's puzzling how they handled it."

"Not all love is meant to last, nor are all connections, and that's not a bad thing. Time and love move as they will, and sometimes the most meaningful ones last the shortest amount of time." I picked something light and upbeat this time, a more recent release that I hadn't seen, hoping to lift Fo's mood. When I settled back in next to him, he seemed tense, distracted.

"Tryst, can I ask you something?"

I paused the movie. "You can ask me anything. I promise."

He fumbled around with the blanket nervously before he

spoke again. "Have you been in love?"

"I thought I was, a couple of times. And I had a long-term boyfriend for a while that I thought might be the love of my life. When we broke up, I was sad for a long time and didn't date anyone. He got married to someone else six months after that, which was a big slap in the face for me." I laughed softly. "It feels like a million years ago now. After that, I stayed withdrawn for a long time. Until I started writing anonymous messages online, looking for connections with people like me."

"That must have been incredibly painful to live through." He found my hand under the blanket and gave it a tentative squeeze.

"It was, but imagine if I'd stayed with him? He was undeniably the wrong person for me, because he wasn't like me in all the important ways. And if I had, we wouldn't have found each other." I squeezed his hand back, firmer than he had, and leaned my head against his shoulder.

"How did you know if it was love or not? You said you thought you were in love several times. What's the difference?"

"Ah, Fo. That's a tough question to answer. Love is hard to understand, and yet so easy sometimes. I think the difference is that I wanted to be in love so much and to be loved that I tried to force those feelings to exist with those other people. It's an easy mistake to make, you know? When you're lonely and need validation, like I was, you can trick yourself into seeing more than what is actually there."

"Oh."

He was quiet for a bit, and I thought it was easy to guess what was on his mind, but I didn't want to rush him to any conclusion. I just stayed still, leaning against him, my heart pounding in my chest. After a couple of minutes, he murmured "okay" then shifted against the pillows so that he could turn to face me, letting go of my hand in the process. I turned, too, so we were face to face. I didn't expect the confession that came next to go the way it did at all.

"I want to be in love with you, Tryst. Maybe that's foolish, a mistake like the ones you made. It's possible I don't actually know what love is, because feelings are something I'm still learning to understand. Whatever this is, maybe it doesn't need to be defined yet. But I can't escape the urge to want to tell you about it; how I want to be near you all the time, and that since we first started talking to each other, you've constantly been on my mind. I think to myself, 'What would Tryst think of this?' and 'I can't wait to talk to her tonight', or I obsess over a million other trivial things that all connect back to you in some way." He reached out and pushed a lock of hair away from my face gently. "I don't know if that's enough to call it love. I don't want to lie to you and tell you that it is when I don't even know how to define love properly.

"But if you walked out of my life now, I'd be devastated. That I know."

In that moment, when my face grew hot with emotion and tears blurred my vision, I knew with blinding clarity that I'd do whatever I could to protect and care for Fo and his open, beautiful heart.

"I—I promise you, I'm not going anywhere." I wiped away some of the tears, a little embarrassed by them, but Fo just smiled fondly and carefully brushed away one that I'd missed.

"Allowing yourself to be vulnerable with me is a gift, Tryst. You don't have to be ashamed of crying. Besides, you've already seen me cry."

"That's true." I couldn't help but chuckle. "We're both an emotional mess."

"I'm new to being a human, at least I have an excuse."

"Did you—did you just *tease* me, Fo?"

When I saw his pleased smirk, I couldn't hold back my laughter.

I was in the middle of a sound sleep, better than I'd had in ages, when I suddenly woke to a shout from Fo. It was dark, and I was disoriented, and that made it all the more terrifying. He was sitting upright in bed, and in the dim light, I could see that his eyes were open, but he didn't seem to register my presence.

At first, I thought he was having a nightmare, although he seemed more angry than scared. It wasn't until I realized that he was twitching, his upper body making small, rhythmic jerks, that it dawned on me that this could be another seizure. It's not like I know much about them; I was relying on the strong vibes my intuition was giving me. I did remember being told once not to try to hold the person having the seizure down or control the seizure, but rather just be there to help keep the person safe until it was over.

I almost jumped out of my skin when Fo grabbed my arm.

"You have to make him stop. He listens to you. He's going to kill me!"

I thought he couldn't be talking to me. He turned to face me directly, and I could see his eyes darting about, as if he were searching the room.

"Trystin. You're the only one who can help me. I know you think I did this to myself, but he—he took me over. That wasn't the plan! Tell him to let me go, let me live, I'm begging you—"

He cut off with a gasp and then slumped forward, all dead weight. I tried to stop his forward tilt with some success, but he weakly pushed me away and let himself fall forward, holding his head in both hands.

"What happened?" He groaned, a chilling sound to me in my emotional state.

"You woke me up, yelling. And then you said some creepy things to me, and…I thought you were having another seizure, but now I'm not sure. Fo, are you okay?" I was suddenly overcome with an urge to cry, but stuffed it down. Later, I told myself. I'd cry later, when we had all this figured out.

"What did I say?" He sat up abruptly, one hand still cupped around his head. "Do you remember?"

"I'm not gonna forget that anytime soon. You said I had to make him stop, that he listens to me, and that he was going to kill you. And—oh shit, I just realized. Fo, you said that you know that I think you did it to yourself. That him taking over wasn't the plan.

"It wasn't you at all, was it? It was Aidan."

He made me recount the entire conversation several times, including how he acted as well as every word he'd uttered to the best of my memory, and with every retelling, he seemed to get more anxious.

"I didn't plan any of this. How can he think that?"

"Can we just stop for a moment and consider this: you thought you'd overwritten him, so how is it that he could come out while you were in some fugue state to beg me to stop you from kicking him out of what appears to be a brain with double occupancy?" It all came out in a breathless tumble, a little sharper than I'd planned, probably because at this point I was exhausted from the drama and being woken up in the middle of the night. I immediately regretted my tone.

"You don't believe me."

"Oh Fo. I'm sorry, I don't mean to be snappy. I'm worried about you and what all this means, and I get crabby when I'm tired. Of course, I believe you; you've never given me reason to doubt you. I'm concerned about what it means that Aidan can hijack you long enough to talk to me. I didn't think he was still a —um—a separate personality from you at this point."

He dropped his head into his hands again, and for a split second, I feared he was going to have another seizure or incident, until I heard his muffled response.

"I'm worried about that too." He took a deep breath, then flopped back on the bed bonelessly, like he'd run out of whatever will had kept him upright to that point. "I thought I understood what happened, but what if I got it all wrong? What if we're both conscious in here, and I'm just overriding him—and what if he *knows* it? Because that's what it sounds like, and I'm completely appalled by what that could mean."

I sank down next to him and found his hand. "No matter what it means, I'm going to keep telling you until it sinks in: *this isn't your fault.* You didn't ask for any of this. It's not like he left instructions or notes or—wait a minute. What if there *are* notes that we could access? Would that help?"

He suddenly sat up and turned on the light next to the bed-couch, momentarily blinding me.

"I don't know if they'd be any help, but Aidan certainly took copious notes. I'm sure all the ones in the labs were destroyed, but he would have kept copies." Just as suddenly as he energized, all that excitement drained away. "But I have no idea where those would be. Here? With my—his—mother? Where would I even start?"

"Well, let me think a minute." I blinked a couple of times, trying to get my eyes to adjust to the room while I ran through possible options. "He doesn't seem like the type who would hide them in a desk, or where you could access them through a desktop link on the laptop. So…hmm."

We both sat there in silence for a few minutes; Fo was deep in thought while I was casting my attention around the room, looking for any kind of clue.

On the surface, Aidan didn't seem to be the kind of guy who needed to hide things much. He lived alone, in a building with good security—but at the same time, his mother had put spy cams everywhere. Either he didn't know, or he did and chose to ignore them.

But I've always believed that everyone needs a secret space, somewhere they can let out all the stuff they're forced to carry with them or stuff down deep inside because saying it aloud would cause more trouble than it was worth. I used to rant in my car when I needed that outlet, before I had my own space. And I've written in a journal because that helps too.

A guy like Aidan—I couldn't see him journaling. If people could get into his place to put in cameras, then there was too much risk that someone would go out of their way to read a journal. And he didn't seem like the writing type.

But a video log? I could see that. As someone doing experiments, that would be a logical leap, at least in my mind.

"When you texted me before you got out of the hospital, you said you had a new device. Is it Aidan's? Is that why it was new to you?"

"Oh. I meant that I had Aidan's device, but of course, I couldn't explain that when I said it to you. It was new to me, because—"

"You'd never had a device before."

We stared at each other, unsure but excited.

"Check your camera and cloud storage, Fo. Maybe we'll get lucky and it'll be that easy."

While he searched, I paced nervously. What if we didn't find what we wanted? What if he recorded lab notes, but they were all clinical and dry, with nothing of his personal thoughts?

Nothing to be done until we knew for sure, I told myself. Stop getting ahead of yourself.

"Tryst? I think I found something."

I plopped back down on the bed next to him, and he pointed to an app in the app list. Something didn't look right to me.

"Data Usage?"

"I searched his apps by 'most used' and this popped up in the top five. There's no way he checked his data usage that often. It has to be a dummy app. It's not on the main screen, so he'd have to go out of his way to open it. Hidden in plain sight."

"Oh! School kids figured that out long ago. Make it look like something else, something boring that everyone has on their device, back when we were still calling them phones. Parents might check your phone for forbidden apps, but they'd see a calculator icon and not even question it or what it hid."

"I'm curious, what kinds of apps would be disallowed?"

"You're trying to distract me from trying to find out if this is what we're looking for, aren't you?" He shrugged, but he had a guilty look on his face. "And the forbidden apps would be chat or video apps. Basically, they'd be looking to control where a kid might go online or what they'd be sharing. Pretty much what Aidan's parents were doing to him, a fully grown man."

"I'm afraid of what we'll find. Or worse, what we won't find." He looked away, his jaw clenching.

"Hey. I can't imagine how difficult all of this is for you. We don't have to try this yet. But Fo, I don't think we can afford to put our heads in the sand about this. I think you might be in danger, in one way or another. Either from your mother or from what we don't know about what happened to you."

"I think 'and' is the proper conjunction there. We know that it's both." I watched his face go through several emotions in succession: anger, frustration, sadness. "I didn't know that being human was going to be this complicated. It seems extremely stressful."

Before I had a chance to respond, he poked the app with a finger, and it opened, filling the screen with...a screen that displayed how much data Aidan's device had used.

"Um, Tryst? I think maybe I was wrong."

"May I see?'

I took the device and scrolled down to the bottom. There was an option labeled "Connections Usage", and on a hunch, I clicked on that. It opened a list of apps with bars under each that showed their data consumption. They were all things you'd expect to see: chat, camera, a search engine, and shopping. Near the end of the list were some service apps, the kind that run in the background to keep the device going. And then there were a handful with no data bars.

"Fo, what about this one?" I pointed out one that was labeled "SysBrain."

"Let's try it."

When he touched the screen, at first it went blank, then a white background with SysBrain in blocky black text appeared. After a moment, the text changed.

SCAN NOW

"What does that mean?" It made no sense to me. But Fo—or maybe the part of Fo that was Aidan—seemed to understand, because he held the device up to his right eye, then his left. There was a quiet click after each time.

ACCESS PERMITTED

The text faded away, replaced by a series of file folders and icons of a mic and camera.

"These folders are all dated, Tryst." I watched him scroll down for what seemed an eternity. "They go back seven years. Wow, he was working on this project for a very long time." His face grew troubled, and his finger, extended over the screen, shook.

"What's wrong?"

"I wonder if that's how long I've been around? I don't know when they took the brain scans, or when he started working on editing and adding what he thought would be improvements. It had to be well before the attempted transfer, right? I remember my first days of truly being aware, but not how long it went before. Or even after; time didn't mean the same things to me while I was only an entity of energy and impulses. Why would it, right?"

I didn't like the edge in his voice. All of this was an unfathomable burden to carry, and I couldn't blame him if the stress of it were beginning to cause cracks to appear. But how do you talk anyone through a trauma like this? I had no point of reference.

"You know, we won't have any clue until we start listening to the logs. We'll figure it out, Fo. We don't have to do it right now, either. We can wait until—"

"No, we can't wait! None of us can," he snapped, and then immediately looked contrite. "Oh, Tryst, I'm so sorry. I feel it, the pressure of *him* inside me, trying to get out, trying to take over. I'm scared, but that's not your fault." He clenched his jaw and wouldn't meet my eyes.

"Look, Fo. I need you to look at me." I waited until he finally, reluctantly, did as I asked. "I'm not taking it personally, okay? You're literally split into two people in there. You're doing the best that you can. I don't love you losing your cool with me, but in this one weird instance, I think it's excusable, okay?"

He slowly nodded, still shamefaced, and I sighed. “I’m sure I’m going to have to say this again in the future, but as long as you’re listening for now, let’s deal with what we’ve got in front of us. Since at least one part of you is insisting, anyway.”

My stomach growled loudly, reminding both of us that though we’d roused while it was still dark, it was now closer to breakfast time than not.

I found eggs in Fo’s refrigerator that surprisingly weren’t too old, and bagels in the freezer. He even had some butter and shredded cheddar that was still fine, so I made scrambled eggs and handed off toasting and buttering bagels to him. His coffee stash was subpar at best, but he had some decent tea, so we were set. He pulled out a big tray from under the bed, and once I dusted it off, it was perfect for our needs.

I took a bite of the bagel and egg sandwich while I convinced his device to cast the contents of the first folder to the big monitor screen we’d been watching movies on earlier.

There were captures of many lab note documents, and two video entries clustered at the bottom of the folder. I’d given the device back to Fo, and he scanned through each document quickly, looking for any clues but not lingering too long on any one of them.

“This is all the preliminaries. Aidan’s going over the basic premise of the work, how they’ve set up the machines that will do the scanning, what he hopes to achieve.” Fo paused, then rubbed his eyes with the back of one hand, being careful to avoid using his buttery fingers. “I noticed he hasn’t said too much about his mother’s goals, just his own. Or maybe the goals of the experiment seem sort of ambiguous to him. I think he’s covering that up by using a lot of technical terms.”

He didn’t need to tell me that; I could read the screen quite well myself and see that I didn’t understand half of what Aidan had typed. Maybe Fo was stressing it so that I didn’t feel stupid for not getting what the notes were saying. It was a nice thought. I can be pretty clever sometimes, but so much of the tech was outside of my wheelhouse.

"I'm going to skip ahead to the videos."

The screen filled up with an image of Aidan and the lab, a bright and well-lit space with a variety of equipment that I didn't recognize. If anything, it made me think of going to the dentist. There was a reclining chair with a strange contraption connected to it. Apparently meant to cover the head, it was shaped like a helmet but with bubbled sections that had wires attached to them. I caught Fo's flinch out of the corner of my eye when he spotted that.

Aidan fascinated me. He looked like Fo, of course—it was the same body—but there were subtle differences. Fo pressed play, and as Aidan walked us around the lab space, he chattered excitedly about the new equipment, their plans to explore improving the human brain, and his role in all of it. He seemed almost effervescent, like a kid who was thrilled for the first day of school or camp, something he'd been waiting to do for a long time.

"You—he—was so young there." I couldn't tear my gaze from the screen. Aidan seemed innocent, joyful. It was evident that he wanted to be part of the team. Thinking about that, it suddenly occurred to me what part of the difference between them might be. "He hasn't talked about being the subject of the experiment at all. I don't think he realized the plan yet."

"No, you're right." I had to strain to hear Fo's voice. It was so low that at first I thought he was talking to himself. "He thought this was the beginning of a new chapter for him, his road to success and pleasing his mother. He didn't know what she'd planned for him. That came later."

The longer we watched Aidan's lab videos, the more a sense of creeping dread, mixed with a deep sadness, took over me. It was affecting Fo, too, but of course it would. Seeing a version of oneself slowly become disillusioned and then bitter and scared? That would do a number on anyone. At first, the videos were all shot in the labs, where Aidan would proudly explain what advances or failures they'd had that day. He had nothing to hide, so the clips were straightforward and usually kept to clinical assessments or notes about what he thought might come of the results.

About a year in, the tone changed.

"It's become clear to me that the goals I'd originally been given have shifted and are no longer in alignment with those I set at the beginning of this work. Thus, the focus of these video notes will also be shifting. We've set out to explore the enhancement of human memory and neural networks through a more hands-on approach, and my notes will begin to reflect my observations both as scientist and subject."

Aidan's voice shook a little as he recorded this, which made me look up from where I'd been staring off into space to focus on the screen. His eyes looked red and puffy, and he was paler than he'd been, although that could have been the lighting. I glanced over to Fo and saw that he was clenching his jaw.

"You okay?"

"Huh?" He visibly made an effort to relax, so I must have made him aware of it. He paused the video before answering me. "I can almost remember these things happening. Or maybe seeing the video is triggering false memories? They're obviously things Aidan went through, so it's possible my mind thinks I should remember them. It's taking everything I've got not to freak out, if I'm being honest."

I carefully moved the big tray to the floor, then slid over next to him. "Is it okay if I rub your shoulders? It won't fix all of this, but it could lessen the tension in your body. You're as taught as a stretched rubber band. I can't imagine that's helping with all of this."

He nodded, little head bobs that did nothing to lessen my impression that he was wound tightly. I moved behind him and put a hand on either shoulder, carefully working the muscles there with my hands. I could feel their tension, but I took it slow, working on being more comforting than therapeutic. I just wanted to put him more at ease for now.

"Aidan was starting to realize how alone he was, how unprotected he was by the people who should have had his best interests at heart before anyone else in the world. And here I am, the result of those betrayals, in his body and his life. The only thing I can call my own is my connection to you, Tryst. I can't begin to explain how that makes me feel." I felt his shoulders begin to loosen under my touch, and his head slumped a little.

"You were screwed over, too. You didn't ask for any of this. I hope you remember that. You're an innocent bystander. Aidan was treated badly, but you know what? He could have walked away. He could have put his foot down."

He sat up straight and pulled away as he turned to face me, a stricken look on his face.

"What if I'm the one to blame for the end results, Tryst? What if I told you that I interfered with the procedure because I didn't want to die? What if—what if I'm the villain of the story after all?"

For just a minute, I thought I'd heard wrong. The villain was Dr. Wood; we both knew that. She was the one who cowed Aidan into being the subject of this ill-advised experiment, the one who tried to control every aspect of Aidan's life—she was undeniably the monster here.

A sinking feeling started in my guts, and uncertainty washed over me in a cold wave. I'd trusted Fo, believed his story completely despite how outlandish it would have been to explain to anyone else, because I'd seen enough proof to substantiate his claims. But the reality of it was that I hadn't seen the *whole* story, had I? It was a puzzle, and I thought I'd assembled enough pieces to see what the finished product would look like, but that was a mistake. I remembered what the Aidan part of him had said to me during that strange dream-state that Fo had gone through.

Am I allowing my feelings to hide the truth about what actually happened?

The gut punch of that thought hurt more than the rest

of it combined. Suddenly, I was reconsidering everything about our time together; what he'd told me or concealed, how Aidan's mother acted when she met me, even the Sui Generis app where we would meet. How did he hide all of this from Aidan? How much did Aidan know about what Fo really was?

Did Aidan or his mother go through with this, knowing that Fo was a thinking, feeling being separate from Aidan?

That last thought jerked me back to the present, where Fo was watching me intently, a mix of fear and resignation on his face.

"You think I'm the villain, too." The way he said it wrenched at my heart.

"There's a lot here I don't understand yet, Fo. But...no. I don't think that." I paused to gather my thoughts and calm myself before I went on. "I think we need to watch the rest of the videos, because there's so much here that we're guessing about. Tell me this: did you honestly interfere with the experiment?"

"Maybe. I think so." He began worrying at the cuticle of his thumb on one hand, nervously picking at it. I'd seen Aidan do the same thing on the video we'd just watched, as he started to talk about the shift in focus.

"You're not sure."

"As...as we were watching the lab reports, I started getting flashes of things. I'm pretty sure they're bits of my memories being triggered, things I've either been unable to access, or I've repressed them. When Aidan started talking about changing his goals, it came back to me in a rush. I said I didn't think I knew what they'd planned for me until much closer to the night of the event, but that's not true. I just didn't want to admit to myself when I had figured it out. And at first I thought they'd, well... that they'd basically clone me and use that to enhance Aidan. And that itself is problematic, but I think they didn't have the capability to do it either."

"They didn't bother to make a backup of you or something? Is that the right terminology?" I felt stupid asking, but I must have said it right because he didn't correct me.

"The kicker is that as far as I know they never bothered to copy my information; maybe they couldn't. Perhaps I got too big and it would have been challenging to contain two of me—that's a strong possibility. I told you that Aidan wasn't paying close attention to me and my growth, probably because he was stressed by the part he had to play in this plan. It was a series of failures. And I think I took advantage of that."

"Did something happen besides the lightning, Fo? What did you do?"

"I haven't quite figured that out." He sighed, resigned. "I guess we need to keep watching these videos until I do."

The farther along we got in the archive, the heavier the atmosphere got—both in the videos and in Fo's apartment. We watched, horrified, as Aidan's entries showed him moving through shock, then anger, and finally a bitter sort of acceptance of the fate his mother had planned for him.

"We did the second brain map today. Mother likes to call it 'landscape mapping' because what we're doing is so much more advanced than the brain or mind mapping of old. Anything she can do to distinguish herself from those scientists of the past and their work. Or to distinguish herself at all, right?"

His sharp laugh was painful to hear.

"I didn't make a recording after the first one. She said it's not supposed to hurt. She's a liar. But it's not like she's tried any of this out on herself, either. I didn't record because I couldn't stop crying. Y'know, there are more ways to inflict pain than through the nerves.

"Anyway, these leave me drained, and there's more to come. She wants to take scans regularly to make sure the maps are up-to-date and accurate. Lucky me."

The next one, dated two weeks after, was even sadder. Aidan had deep circles under his eyes.

"I'd be okay with reliving all the high points if I didn't have to go through all the lows, too. It's not even reliving. It's just all raw emotions."

He ran a hand through his coppery hair, a habit I'd seen Fo do many times.

"Third brainscaping. Scraping. I wonder if the damn program feels any of this, or if it gets to be me without the highs and lows? Aidan 2.0, now fully improved to be the perfect son and subject without pain or regret. Maybe without morals? I guess that'd be an improvement for what they want from me."

I glanced over and saw Fo sitting upright, unmoving, his eyes fixed on his twin on the screen. Him, but not.

"We can take a break, you know." I tried to say it in the most neutral voice I could manage. I didn't want to push either way or assume that I knew what he needed. I wouldn't know how to feel or what to do if our situations were reversed.

"I can't access all the memories he had to experience repeatedly, at least not yet. But I know pain. And regret. He suffered much to lose it all in the end."

"It's not your fault."

"I keep telling myself that, but you know I can't fully believe it. That's why I can't take a break yet. I need to know the truth."

We kept watching. I did make him stop so we could shower, telling Fo that it would give us time to digest what we'd already seen and refresh us. He argued half-heartedly with me but gave in, then admitted when he came out after his turn, hair damp and rumpled, that he did feel a little better. I wanted him to take a nap or at least look at something else for a while, but he couldn't be deterred.

"She's started compiling the scrapes. Patchworking all the versions of me together to make as close a replica of a complete me as possible. Once that's done, it'll be my turn to teach myself how to fill up the expanded brain space. Never wanted a kid, and now I get to raise myself, what a trip."

Again, that barking, sarcastic laugh.

"I'm starting out with a sandbox environment where I can

pre-load enrichment and do progress testing. Once I get the completed compile, we'll go on to the next steps. I keep telling her that this thing is going to be a resource hog, and she just asks me if I want to be smarter, because that's what it requires. Like what I want is even part of the equation at this point."

The next recording was a week later. Aidan looked a little lighter and fresher than he had in the past few videos, which was a bit of a surprise.

"I have to admit that watching the construct develop has been rewarding. If I manage to think about it as an entity separate from myself, that is. The urge to give it a cute nickname is strong, and I'm not sure what that says about me other than I'm human and we'll bond with anything, even ourselves."

For once, the laugh that followed was light, genuine. It's the closest I've seen Aidan and Fo's personalities reflect each other. That ease didn't last, sadly.

"If only I could convince Mother to let this continue as a closed environment experiment instead, or even one where the construct was allowed to live out a free existence housed in our lab framework…we already have enough breakthrough results to write a dozen papers. The potential of this work has hardly been tapped.

"My next task is expanding the sandbox. And figuring out how to address my twin consciousness beyond calling it "the construct" or "Aidan 2.0" because that's reserved for—well, you know. Later."

"Sandbox? That's a limited workspace, right?" I knew the term, but I wasn't entirely sure about what it meant. Programming isn't my thing.

"Right. It keeps programs isolated, so they can only interact with other things permitted into the sandbox. They wanted me to be able to consolidate myself and start growing in an environment that was safe for both them and me. If my data touched something with corruption or interacted with a virus at that point, everything would have been over. And they couldn't risk me going out into the bigger world of the Internet yet. I wasn't ready."

"That makes sense. You were still a baby, in a manner of speaking."

Fo frowned, but nodded. "As much as I hate thinking of it like that, you're right. I was essentially helpless and in need of a lot of growth. At that point, I needed protection and guidance."

"Did you get it? Aidan sounds more invested in the project at this point."

"I did. Once I was fully integrated and learned how to think properly, I began to understand that the ones who spoke to me were my creators, and they encouraged me to learn and grow. They provided me with endless games and educational programs, which I had to finish before I was allowed to move into supervised interaction with less closed systems. I didn't understand at first that the 'voices' were Aidan and his mother. Or that they were the ones to engineer my existence, and plan my end use."

"You must have been so confused in the beginning. When did you begin to feel like you understood things?"

Fo snorted, a bitter sort of amusement that sounded more like an Aidan response. "I'm not sure I can claim that even now, Tryst. Every time I think I'm beginning to get a grip on everything that's happened, there's another surprise thrown my way."

"I get that. It's so much to take in."

"That's my life now, I guess." He shrugged, a gesture that I knew was a lie. "At least I'm not living it out trapped in a sandbox, because eventually I would have figured out that there was so much I was missing."

He slouched over, looking down at the floor instead of me or the screen, and I suddenly wanted to hug him fiercely. What a bullshit stacked deck of cards he'd been forced to pull from.

"Hey Fo?" He looked up and forced a small smile for me. That hit me right in the guts. "You're here with me now. You're free. Let's see what we can do to understand what happened, and maybe you can move forward from there. It's clear to me that none of this can be laid at your feet. Do you believe me?"

"I don't know how free I am, not really. But for you, I'll try and believe that."

Never in my life have I wanted to punch someone in the face more than I wanted to punch his mother. If Aidan was half the same as Fo, she had a better son than she ever deserved.

We watched more of the videos. Aidan's mood went up and down, but the closer we got to the end date, the more frustrated and panicky he sounded. It was plain to see that he knew the end was near.

"Construct is progressing much faster than predicted. It has absorbed all the information we have allowed access to and stated that it is bored.

Bored. *I know it's a good sign, but that word makes me want to punch things. We're keeping an intelligence locked up and stifled, when it's blatant that it requires the very thing it was designed for, more information. And it's a sign that we'll be moving to stage two soon."*

Aidan's delivery of the next entry was emotionless. His face was not.

"Construct has progressed to a stage where we feel confident in unfettered access to the Internet. We equipped it with programming to assist in the avoidance of malware and other compromised data, and stressed that safety protocols must be followed at all times for the good of itself and the mission at hand."

Aidan drew closer to the camera, his voice almost a whisper.

"It knows. It knows what the plan is.

I don't think it meant to give that away, but it isn't very skilled at lying or hiding things from me. I can't decide if this makes it easier or harder. I guess it takes away one burden and replaces it with a different, equally shitty one. Sorry that I gave it life only to take it away by squishing it back into my head. Which, by the way, no one is sure either of us will survive. If it were up to me, I'd find a way to set it free and let it roam the Internet forever. But the data's tied to our servers, and the only one who has the ability to sever that is Mother. And she's not going to just do that and give up on her dreams, either version of my life be damned.

"The more I learn about our Construct, the more I wish we could have been friends instead of whatever this twisted relationship is. It's a version of me that was never allowed to be."

"It loves astronomy and poetry. It doesn't know that I know it, but it programmed a virtual world for itself, based on a place I love the most. It's been sending messages to strangers in hopes of connection because I can't be the one to give it—him—the love he craves."

Fo's voice overlapped Aidan's, a perfect echo of his thoughts confessed to an audience that he never knew he would have.

"...Fo?"

"I remember this. I remember it, Tryst. Not my memories, his. Ours, now. And I remember how he felt, the fear and regret and *amazement* that I'd come from him but was myself, and the guilt that came from that realization." He shoved his hair away from his forehead, agitated. "He knew I was a person. Autonomous, alive on my own terms. He knew, and he tried to tell his mother, and she laughed in his face."

"Oh my god."

"She denied that it was true. But he believed that it wouldn't matter either way; maybe she knew the truth, or not, but she wouldn't stop."

He stood up abruptly, surprising me with the sudden decisiveness of motion, then just as suddenly sank back down into his seat, all but collapsing as he let his breath out in a loud sigh.

"There's one more left. We should finish this."

He tapped the play button, and Aidan's voice filled the room.

"She's decided that tomorrow is the big day. All the tests we've run on the Construct indicate that now is the best time to integrate it into the host. And me, that host? I'm in top condition for this proced-

ure, too. She's basically kept me captive in order to monitor me. Or to keep me from running away, I suppose. I decided a while ago that the wisest thing I could do was play along with it, not fight back or argue with her. Despite everything, I still wanted to see how this would play out. And now here we are, at the end of this stage, the final chapter before two lives are crushed into one despite the wishes of either of us, and I have regrets about my lack of resistance.

No matter, though. I have a plan."

He looked around the room nervously, then leaned close to the camera.

"I hope that everything I've recorded here sheds light on the experiment when all is said and done. The fault is mine, and mine alone. I'm not sure what will happen to me, or the Construct. If all goes as planned, this will be the first and last time this experiment will happen. I've set the parameters for catastrophic system failure, and if I've timed it right, that will make sure that no one can attempt this again. At least it won't happen for a long time, given that the calculations and equipment we have here are destroyed.

"I don't care if she doesn't forgive me. I can't forgive myself for allowing this to go on. The real tragedy here is the Construct. May it not suffer for long."

The video stopped, frozen on Aidan's resolute face. I turned to Fo and saw it mirrored there on the face he shared, alongside so much more, with Aidan.

"He did it. The lightning had nothing to do with disrupting the procedure, nothing at all. He triggered the system to completely shut down during the process, but his timing was off; it was too late to stop the transfer. It was too late." Fo ran his hand through his rumpled hair again, and I realized he might be trying to soothe himself in the only way he knew how. His low voice quivered as he continued. "The lightning just hid his tracks. It was a lucky strike."

"He planned to kill you both to end the experiment." It felt unfathomable to me.

"I don't know if he knew what the results would be, beyond corrupted. He risked scrambling his brains and living with that for the rest of his life. He risked destroying me. He wanted to make sure his mother couldn't do this to anyone else, and that was the only possible avenue he saw. I don't know if he was a fool or a hero. Or—if I could have made that choice."

"You are from Aidan. I think you would have."

"Would I?" He worried his lower lip between his teeth for a moment, thinking. "I don't think so. I was afraid of dying, whatever that meant for me in that form. I feared the act of being reunited with Aidan and losing my autonomy, but I have to admit that a part of me yearned for the ability to have a body and freedom from the online world. And more? To see you, face to face. To have the possibility to touch you, if that were an option. I let that give me hope, despite knowing that it meant possible catastrophe for both myself and my host. That was what kept me going. And somehow, I ended up in this brain as the dominant persona. Aidan is in here, but..."

"But?"

"Despite his best efforts, I don't think he will come to the forefront again." He met my gaze, then looked away, as if it was too much scrutiny to bear. "I think he told us what he needed to, and now he's willing to sink into the recesses of this mind we share. Or perhaps we're destined to integrate finally. I could see that as a possibility; I have had more of his memories surface as we've watched these videos."

"Are you both going to be okay with that?" I don't know what made me ask it. It just slipped from me. He didn't answer right away, and when he did, his voice was so soft I had to strain to hear it.

"I think we will."

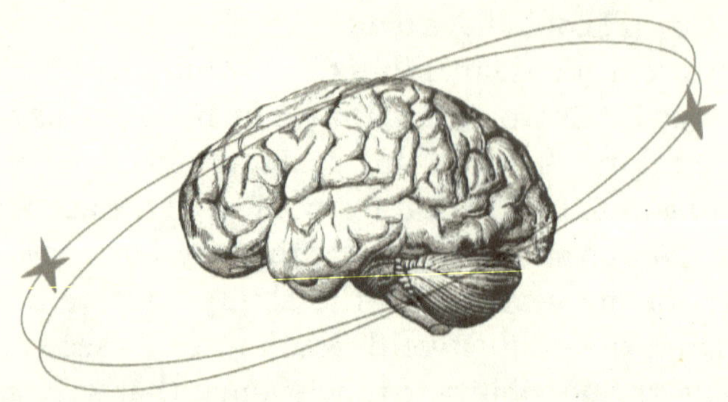

CHAPTER EIGHT

I didn't know what to say after that, and Fo looked like he needed some time to think—I can't say that I blamed him. After a few awkward minutes, I decided that maybe giving him some space would be smart.

"Hey, why don't I go home and grab some clothes, maybe pack a bag, then I can come back and we can figure out what we want to do next?" I tried to sound upbeat and partially succeeded.

"I can go with you."

"You can, but maybe you need some alone time. You just had a lot of information dumped in your lap, right?"

He considered the suggestion, then reluctantly nodded. "You're probably right. You know more about how to be human than I do. You have the door code, right?"

I did. Fo walked me to the door, trailing behind me, but before I could leave, he pulled me into a tight hug.

"I'm glad it was you here with me today. Thank you for being so understanding. I know this is overwhelming. You didn't sign up for being with a strange experiment of a guy."

"You didn't sign up for being an experiment, either." I leaned hard into the hug, hoping that he could soak up all the comfort I could give.

The sun was starting to set lower in the sky by the time I finished packing a bag with clothes and toiletries. I also took the time to shower and change my clothes, because I felt like I needed a mental reset.

I took my time walking back, stopping to enjoy some of the late-season flowers still blooming in the tiny neighborhood gardens. I wasn't avoiding going there, not exactly. I just needed to look at something pretty while I let myself get back into the right headspace to deal with the repercussions from what we learned from the ghost of Aidan.

I probably shouldn't think of him like that, but damn if it didn't feel like Fo was haunted by him. It was a weight that Fo would carry for a long time, if not the rest of his life. I could punch Aidan's mother in the face for that, too. I swear I'm not a violent person, but when I thought about what she put her own flesh and blood through for her ambition, I got a hot flash of anger that made me want to hit things.

There was a part of me that I didn't want to acknowledge, which was also angry because I'd finally found someone who liked me for who I am. Then it turned out that he'd been loaded down with an unbelievable amount of mental baggage—and not the usual kind, but something out of a sci-fi movie. I couldn't even talk to anyone about it, because who would believe me? At least he had someone he could lean on who knew he was telling the truth. Imagine having to deal with it without having someone in his court?

We were stuck with each other. Good thing he seemed happy to be stuck with me. And me? As weird as the situation was, I couldn't imagine walking away, not at this point. He was my Fo. We'd shared parts of ourselves that no one else knew. He'd trusted me with his deepest secrets. There was no way I was going to leave him to face the future on his own.

Even if part of that was confronting his mother.

Did that thought make it happen? I'm not superstitious, even though Mamá is, and I was surrounded by those kinds of thoughts my whole life. She would have cautioned me about calling my fears into being.

The front door to the building was open when I got there.

That in itself didn't set off too many warning bells, because one of the other tenants could have left it that way, despite the clear desire for building security, what with the keypad entry and front door cameras.

Or maybe the cameras were from his mother, too.

That thought made me begin to worry, and I rushed up to Fo's unit as fast as I could.

That door was open, too. Fo's hoodie was lying on the ground, and the sleeve had kept the door from fully closing.

"Fo! Fo? Oh, please be here."

The place didn't look like there'd been a struggle, at least. Nothing was knocked over or out of place at first glance, and if the door hadn't been left ajar, I wouldn't have thought twice about it. Maybe I would have guessed that he'd stepped out to get some snacks or take a walk to clear his head.

But he would never have left that hoodie. He practically lived in it.

My device, in the pocket of my hoodie, made a noise. It had been a while since I'd heard it, so it took a moment for me to recognize the soft chime that signaled there was a message in the Sui Generis app.

I fumbled trying to get the damn thing out of my pocket, almost dropping it in my panic. It took what felt like a million years to open the app and then for it to load. Finally, the field opened, dappled late afternoon sunlight on the long grasses, dazzling me before the text box appeared, along with the glowing orb that represented Fo.

`Don't panic. She has me, but Thomas is here. He's waiting for the right moment. And I'll give him my device.`

There was another ping, and when I swiped down to see what it was, a question box popped up.

`YOU HAVE A REQUEST TO CONNECT: YES/NO`

I tapped "yes", and a map opened. There was a dot for me, and one that was moving away, headed away from me, out of the city on I-83.

```
Meet Thomas here? Carefully. No car. Soon.
```

The text box remained, but Fo's avatar disappeared.

Here, he said. Of course not in the app; he meant at the field where we'd stargazed. I assumed that the road that led to the field had cameras, so I'd have to find a place to park the Jeep and walk in. Fine, I could do that.

I took a couple of minutes to splash water on my face, and then I took off my hoodie and put Fo's on, just for comfort and strength. It was loose on me, which was ridiculous since he was so much thinner than I was, but he did like his clothes kind of baggy. I dumped all my extra clothes out of the backpack, put my own hoodie in, grabbed the snacks on the counter, and a bottle of water. No telling how long I'd need to wait, and Fo might need food after all of this, too. If I could manage to rescue him.

No, I wasn't going to think like that. I *would* rescue him.

The drive felt like it took an excruciatingly long time, and I could feel my anxiety bubbling under the surface despite all my efforts to push it back down. I usually listen to music when I'm driving, but not that day. I think I would have started screaming if anything Fo and I had listened to came up on my playlist.

I slowed down once I was in the area of Fo's meadow, looking for anywhere appropriate that I could stash the Jeep. There was a road that turned off to the left before the entrance, and I took that, hoping for something, anything. When I spied the sign for a popular-looking tavern, with a half-full parking lot, I pulled in. It was easy to hide the Jeep at the back of the lot, camouflaged by the bigger SUVs of rich people. Hopefully, it would stay that way. It was getting dark enough now that chances were good no one would notice if it was there for a while.

I waited until there wasn't anyone else in the parking lot before I slipped into the woods and started hiking to the meadow. Thankfully, it wasn't too overgrown or difficult, though I did trip on some vines a couple of times, and stumbled once into a tree, scraping the palm of my right hand. It was more annoying than anything, but it was a reminder to be careful.

I walked parallel to the road, but at a hidden distance, until I saw the open field through the trees. How was I going to do this? I was supposed to meet Thomas, but I couldn't just walk out into the meadow and look for him; I had no clue if I'd be spotted by the wrong people. I had his number—what if I texted him?

`Thomas, I'm here. Carefully. What do I do?`

It took a minute—an eternity—to get his response.

`Wait where you are. I'll find you.`

Was I that easy to spot? Hopefully, no cameras had picked me up. I had tried so hard to be sneaky. There just wasn't any way to know where they were, so it was a guessing game at best.

There was a log down, conveniently placed where I could stay sheltered behind a bush, but could still see some of the open space not far away. I hunched over, elbows on knees, probably looking as miserable as I felt. What the hell was I going to do to help Fo? What did I possibly have to offer in a situation like this? Other than my rage at how his mother was treating him, I guess. I was getting angrier by the moment. And cold. The temp out there, so close to water, was falling rapidly. And it was getting darker by the second.

I heard a noise off to my right, a slight crunch of leaves, and whirled to see what it was. A catbird looked back at me from the branch of a sassafras, almost hidden by its bright yellow leaves. It stared at me for a moment, called out with that distinctive mewing sound that they make, then flew off.

"Ms. Morales." The deep voice behind me wasn't much more than a whisper, thankfully, or I might have shot off into space.

"You startled me!" I kept my voice as quiet as possible, but I let my face telegraph my dismay.

"Not my intention, I promise. We don't have much time, so listen carefully. I can get you into the house; no one will be watching the cameras unless the perimeter alarms are tripped, and those are only at the gates, fence, and other entrances. I will help you pass through the rear gate safely." He gestured beyond the meadow. "We'll stay hidden until we get to that gate. It never hurts to be extra cautious. But Ms. Morales, what is your plan once you are inside?"

"I have no idea. Hopefully, I get some ideas once the shit starts going down, I guess."

"Your honesty is refreshing, but it's also alarming. You need a plan, Tryst."

Using my given name caught me off guard. That was a first.

"I know. I am so out of my element, Thomas. I don't know what I'm doing. I'm scared and out of my depth. But I'm all Fo's got. Me and you." I scuffed the fallen leaves in front of me with a toe. "If I have to go in punching, I will. But maybe I'll be able to talk my way through this. I have no idea what to expect, so I'm just going to go with the flow and hope that I'm clever enough to come up with a winning plan."

Thomas frowned and shook his head, extending a hand to pull me up from my seat on the fallen log. "You're a brave one. I hope that's enough."

I followed close behind—him incongruous in his fine black suit, me in my scruffy joggers and hoodie, as mismatched as could be—through the trees until we arrived at the gate. It wasn't fancy, more like the kind you see on farms, made to let animals or work vehicles through. Judging by the tracks in the mud on our side of the gate, probably ATVs used it more than anything else.

"Wait here." He moved out into the open. I could barely make it out as he waved his arm over a box attached to the gate.

There was a clicking noise, and it swung open slightly. I thought he might gesture for me to come over, but instead, he came back to me.

"Stick close to me, like a shadow." He grabbed my arm and tugged, and I hustled to keep up as he practically dragged me through the gate, closing it after. He kept that up until we rounded a bend in the path and couldn't see the gate anymore. "We should be good now."

"No cameras from here?" I rubbed my arm where he'd pulled on it.

"Sorry, didn't mean to hurt you. I didn't want to give them any reason to look closely. Not that it would be easy now that the sun's down." He reached into a pocket and pulled out a black band. "Here, put this on. It registers with my code and opens all doors on the property. And yes, there will be cameras once we're at the house, but they aren't usually monitored unless someone's near without one of these on. The system monitors the transponders."

"But—won't it notice that there are two of you roaming about?"

"Ah, I'm way ahead of you. I gave you my band. I have another one with me, registered to the staff. I will be fine, Ms. Morales."

"Of course. You're a professional."

He honest-to-god laughed at my joke. "I'm glad you understand that." The smile didn't last long, fading away with his next words. "I've been with Aidan for a long time. My job is to protect him, even from his own family. They've made it very difficult for me to do that recently. Truth is, I failed him, and now it's on me to correct that, at least as much as possible."

"How much do you know about what happened?" We were getting close to the house now, and I needed to get all the info that I could before we couldn't talk anymore.

"Enough to know that it didn't go as planned, and that something happened with Aidan." He sighed, then paused for a moment, with what I thought was an attempt to choose the right words. "His personality didn't change exactly, but something inside did. And it's apparent that he had some kind of secret life that even I didn't know about until the accident." He gestured at me, visibly frustrated at his lack of foreknowledge.

"What if I told you that it wasn't him but a sort of electronic copy of him that knew me? And that his mother's experiment was to paste that copy over the Aidan that you knew?"

He stopped dead in his tracks and turned to stare at me, or as much as he could see of me.

"I'm no scientist, but that's crazy talk."

"Neither am I, but I saw the lab notes that Aidan left. What do you know about what was going on?"

"It was an enhancement treatment, designed to help increase memory and retention and—oh."

I didn't say anything else, just stood there with my hands in my hoodie pockets. I wanted to give him time to think through everything and come to his own conclusion.

"That soulless bitch!"

I would have feared for my life if the anger in his voice had been directed at me.

"Yeah. We need to rescue him before something worse happens. I don't know what her plan is, and I'm not sure Fo did either. Aidan, I mean."

"No, if he wants to be called Fo now, that's his name. Let's go get him."

The house was huge, a well-lit bulk of red brick and white trim that screamed money. The yard behind it featured a covered patio and a large pool—of course there was a pool—and a separate multi-bay garage with a long driveway that curved around the building and disappeared. All pretty much what I expected from rich people; very much not my scene. I tried to imagine Aidan growing up here, but I failed. It was so unlike either what I knew of him or the Fo I knew now as to feel alien.

We stayed to the outside edge of the yard, moving behind the garage and across the driveway until we reached the flagstone-covered space in front of the rear entrance. We climbed the steps, flanked by ornamental shrubs, and Thomas opened the door to let me through.

We were in.

We'd walked into a large sunroom-type space, all white and with an open plan, the kind of place where rich people might lounge with fancy drinks. I say this knowing nothing about how wealthy people live, of course, because I'd only seen places like this in shows or movies. The closest I'd come to this in real life was a high-end hotel in DC I walked through once, on a dare.

Thomas silently pointed to our left and led me through the fanciest kitchen I'd ever seen. Again, everything was white, or the kind of steel that would show marks if you looked at it wrong. It was professional grade, actually nicer than any kitchen I'd ever worked in, and spotless. It looked like no one ever actually cooked in there, but I would bet money that they had a private chef. It was definitely that kind of vibe.

On the other side of the kitchen was a swinging door that led to a rather plain hallway, very different from what I'd seen so far, and this I understood. They had separate spaces for the staff, because of course, who wants to interact with the riff-raff that serves you, am I right? No wonder this house was so big; it needed to conceal all these extra corridors.

Gross.

However, it was good for us as we were able to move through the house without being seen. I didn't even see evidence of cameras in the hallway. Thomas led me through, passing by several doors I assumed opened into downstairs rooms until we reached a staircase at the end. It was steep, with risers that were higher than those on regular stairs. Of course, that was to minimize space used, even if that made it more difficult for the help.

Somehow, I managed to get to the top without making too much noise, though I was out of breath. Thomas, of course, didn't even look winded, but I guess if you used them often, you'd be in great shape.

That's when I started hearing raised voices, muffled at

first but growing in intensity as we edged down the hall to a room near the end of the passageway. I immediately recognized Fo's voice, even before I could discern what was being said.

"Your actions could have thrown away countless hours of work, you fool." That was Mrs. Wood's voice, bitter and accusing.

Fo said something in return, but he was practically mumbling, and I couldn't make out anything he was saying. I glanced at Thomas, and he shook his head ever so slightly.

"You keep saying I don't understand, but I've given you every chance to explain, Aidan. This nonsense about making a mistake is something that I thought we covered long ago. You agreed to this work, and until recently, I thought we were on the same page. And then the storm happened, and that *woman* conveniently appears when it's obvious that you've been distracted —and all you can say to me is that it's a mistake?"

"Let the man talk, Clarissa."

That was a new voice, one I didn't know. I saw one of Thomas' eyebrows raise, then his forehead creased, and he got a guarded look. I didn't know what that could mean, but I didn't like it.

"If only he'd say something of *use*, Stephen, but he's not giving me any reason to listen to his repeated excuses—"

"Darling. You've asked a lot of him. Too much, perhaps. He had a big scare and wanted to live a little. He's here now, though, right?" There was a pause, and I wished dearly that I could see into the room right then. "Son, take your time. Explain it to us when you're ready."

This time I could hear Fo a little more clearly. "It didn't work correctly. I've been trying to tell you. There was an anomaly. The experiment's been compromised."

Mrs. Wood snorted, and even from the other side of the wall, I could hear the skepticism in her retort. "You were struck by lightning, of course, it's been compromised! But I assure you that the transfer went as planned. And here you are, already recovered and performing perfectly well. Even if you've shown me that you're undependable."

Again, there was some incoherent mumbling from Fo, and then I heard a thump, closely followed by a gasp from his mother.

"What is this? Get up, get up—Stephen, what's happening to him?"

I heard some rustling and a series of small thuds, and I knew what the deal was even without seeing it. Fo was having another seizure.

I was flooded with a nauseating rush of panic, and without thinking, I scrambled for the door, jerked it open, and practically fell into the room, Thomas close on my heels.

"Move, move," I spat out, pushing my way past Mrs. Wood to get to Fo's side. I didn't know what I was doing, but there was no way I wasn't going to be next to him. I dropped to my knees and started whispering in his ear, desperate to reach him in this fugue state and bring him back.

"Fo! I'm here, it's Tryst. You need to calm down; you have to come back. It's okay, it's okay. I'm here next to you. I promised I'd be by your side. Come back and you'll see. I'm always here for you, Fo."

Miraculously, the tremors began to slow, then ceased. Fo didn't open his eyes right away, but his hand found mine and he gave it a weak squeeze.

"You found me."

"I told you. I promised. I keep my promises."

"Tell them. Tell them what happened, Tryst. I can't right now." His words slurred at the end, but I felt like he wasn't in danger of seizing again, at least not at that moment.

I stared at his face for a moment longer, scanning every detail. I told myself that I wanted to make sure he was truly okay before I started speaking—but looking back at it, I think I was afraid that something bad was going to happen, and I needed to memorize it in case I lost him forever.

"You forced him to kill a version of himself, you ghoul," I spat out, unable to hold back the vitriol that had been growing steadily inside me. "You pushed Aidan even when he knew something bad was happening with the experiment. You guilted him into being a guinea pig, and then when he had doubts about what was happening with the Construct, you ignored him."

"What on Earth are you talking about?" She looked as if I'd slapped her. "Aidan came into this under his own free will. When he started to get cold feet, we'd already invested too much into this to stop, so of course, I talked him down. We can't be letting our *emotions* get in the way of scientific advancement. And how would you know what concerns he had, or even what this is all about? Surely you're not hiding an advanced degree in a pocket somewhere?"

"No need to be condescending to the girl, Clarissa—"

"The duplicate became autonomous." Fo cut off his father with the blunt statement. He forced himself to prop himself up and locked eyes with his mother. "We did not integrate properly. There are...consequences."

"What?" Both the Woods exclaimed at the same time, and Mrs. Wood's face suddenly paled.

"Oh, now you care," I muttered, and slid over to help bolster Fo while he struggled to stay upright. "There are two versions of him stuck in one head, and neither one of them trusted you enough to tell you. It's been us trying to figure out things all this time."

"But how?"

"Oh, that's *fascinating.*"

The overlapping reactions were too much. I didn't trust either parent, but at least Aidan's father hadn't spoken about him like he was a test subject.

"I knew you were acting erratically, but I assumed that was aftereffects from the lightning strike. But tell me, am I speaking with Aidan now? Or..." Her eyebrow raised, and all my internal alarms started going off at her expression. "Is this the Fo I've heard so much about who is here with us?"

"You don't need to answer her." I gripped his arm, squeezing it to reinforce my opinion.

"We are both here. Fomalhaut is the dominant entity, so

you can consider your experiment failed in that aspect, as it was designed to reinforce the original programming, not overwrite or corrupt it. But Aidan is still a resident in the system."

The way he explained it to his mother made all the sense in the world. But the words he used were so cold, so clinical—no, I knew what it was. They reminded me of when Fo and I started talking, how stiff his speech would be sometimes before he figured out how other people casually spoke to each other and grew more comfortable with it. Which of course I hadn't known at the time was happening, but with this reversion, it was unmistakable.

What I didn't understand was why.

"My son is a resident. In his own body and mind."

I turned to look at Mr. Wood, and in that instant, I became sure of his place in all of this. He was the kind who wore his emotions on his face, much like the videos of Aidan had shown about his own personality. In fact, they looked so much alike that there was no doubt that Aidan took after him.

"You didn't know anything about what was planned, did you?"

"This is Ms. Morales, sir. She's the one I told you about."

I turned to stare at Thomas. "You told him about me?"

"Who do you think had me make sure you arrived home? I told him about you as soon as I dropped you off at the hospital room." He surprised me then by looking as close to embarrassed as I think he was able. "Though everything else has been of my own choice. I appreciate how steadfast you've been. Aidan's been under my watch for a while now, so I needed to know that about you. And it was my job to share that with Mr. Wood."

"I see that, Thomas." Mr. Wood waved his hand in a dismissive gesture. "We can explain all of our parts in Aidan's life later, but first I need to ask my wife a pressing question: What the hell were you thinking?"

A small whimper escaped me as he went from upset to furious in the blink of an eye. Thank fucking god that energy wasn't focused on me. Thankfully, Fo's hand moved to rest on my thigh protectively—not that he was in any shape to protect me from anything—and that helped me get myself back together. The volatile uncertainty of the situation was wearing me down.

"What do you mean, Stephen? What was I thinking? That not only could this process be an advancement for humankind, it could change everything." She dropped her arms from where they'd been crossed over her chest and stared at her husband meaningfully. "It could be a cure. We could bring you back to yourself."

"Oh my god, Clarissa." He pressed two fingers to his forehead with a pained look, then looked away from her with a clenched jaw.

"Isn't that what you want? To have your life back? Your mind?" She put her hands on the desk that he was sitting behind, leaning forward so that she was almost at his level.

Almost.

"You know very well that I do. But not at the cost of our son's life, or his mind."

"It was his idea, Stephen."

...What?

I turned to Fo and saw my skepticism echoed there, slowly fade, and turn into recognition.

"That's—that's not entirely true."

"What is she talking about, Fo?"

"Aidan." He paused, his eyes darting rapidly around the room for a moment as if he was looking for the right words to show up in front of him. "Aidan thought that it would be a much less rigorous process. One that would simply enhance his brain without much fuss. He trusted his mother's work in the beginning; she's always been brilliant, and she had a good reason to pursue this research, just as Aidan did to volunteer."

I looked at Mrs. Wood, then to her husband, taking the time to take in his appearance beyond his resemblance to Aidan. His sunken eyes, the weakness of his hands when he'd gestured. The fact that he hadn't moved from the chair he was in.

"You've had CAIRS. That's why you can't work anymore. That's why your wife is the one running the labs."

Cascading AutoImmune Respiratory Syndrome, or CAIRS, was a short-lived but devastating pandemic that had shut down everything in a way that hadn't been seen in the US since COVID in 2020. Unlike that one, the government and WHO had taken quicker steps to isolate its spread. Still, it had taken a toll on the medical establishment and caregivers, killing as many as it left disabled, and reducing the healthcare industry significantly for a while.

The condition had several hallmark aftereffects; besides the debilitating fatigue and weakness, the inflammation that it caused in the body left a lingering toll on the mind. Some were lucky to be left with intermittent brain fog, but the worst cases found that they were locked out of significant portions of their memory and recall. The way I'd read one sufferer describe it was "as if a wall stood between my knowledge and my consciousness." The consensus was that something had happened to disconnect those parts of the mind, or weaken the connections considerably.

"The singular solution they were looking for was to bypass the damage in your brain. All of this was designed to help you."

"That's not all of it." Fo stood up, pushing himself up off the floor with a bit of a struggle at first. He extended a hand to me, but I shook my head and got up on my own.

"What else is there?" Mr. Wood's face was unreadable, emotionless.

"Why don't you explain it, Mother? Because it's your plan, after all."

Mrs. Wood snorted. "And because you only guessed at it and don't know all the details, you mean. But yes, I admit that there's more to be gained from this work than just a possible workaround for post-CAIRS damage. We're seen from the tragically corrupted attempt and unification that it is possible to make the procedure work, though there will be much to analyze before we can go further." She turned to pin Fo with a sharp look. "But despite attempts to keep the true nature of the union with Aidan and the Construct a secret from me post-experiment, I knew as soon as he gained consciousness in the lab that I was not speaking to the Aidan that I knew. I didn't understand the situation was quite like *this*, but I knew something had gone off script."

"He spoke to you? I thought he was unconscious before they got him to the ER!" Aidan's father was too weak to manage a shout, but he jerked forward into the desk with a bang as the arms of his chair connected with the dark wood.

"He won't forgive you. And neither will I. That's what Aidan said. And it *was* your son—Aidan, and I are both your son —even though you don't want to hear that."

I watched Mrs. Wood's self-assured expression slip for just a moment when Fo quietly dropped those words into the conversation like a well-timed bomb. Despite everything, did she have regrets?

"I'm not asking for forgiveness from either of you. We've achieved breakthroughs beyond anything we imagined, any of us." She glanced at her husband, and I saw that quick slip in her resolve again before she schooled her face. "Do you realize what this means, that we have been able to replicate the mind of a living person in a virtual setting? Imagine the possibilities!"

"But he's not a replica! Fo is a distinct being, twinned off but with his own personality and mind. And that's why the initial experiment failed." I couldn't keep from clenching my fists; I was so angry. I could feel myself vibrating from the emotions coursing through me. "You tried to cram two people into one mind. And I think you knew that was a possibility and you went ahead with the trial anyway, because you *didn't want to stop.*"

Before she could protest, Fo added, "Aidan didn't want to do it. He was terrified at the end. He understood the possible ramifications. And so did I. He was the one to corrupt the uploading process, and it was only by luck that the storm covered his tracks. Unfortunately—or quite fortunately from the point of my existence—he was too late to stop my introduction into his network."

"But why didn't Aidan put a stop to it before it got to that point?" Mr. Wood ran a shaking hand through his hair, a gesture I'd seen Fo do a million times. "Why didn't he just say no if he knew that the experiment was ethically compromised?"

"Because he didn't feel like he could speak up? Because it was supposed to be something to help save his father, who he loves—and it was run by his mother, who he fears? I mean, those reasons alone are enough to mess with anyone's resolve, but what do I know?" I couldn't seem to control the bitter, sarcastic tone, but at this point, I was just done with the lack of care that had been shown to either Aidan or Fo. "Isn't anyone worried about the effects this has had on him? He had a seizure right in front of you, and it's not the first, and here we are arguing about the *importance* of this *fucking experiment.*"

Fo put a hand on my arm, squeezing it gently.

"It's okay, Tryst. Aidan knew what to expect, and so do I. That's why he sabotaged the systems, to keep the research from going any further, at least for a while."

"Oh. This reminds me of why I brought you here in the first place. What a needless amount of destruction the two of you did." An unpleasant aura of self-satisfaction oozed from her, and I did not like the implication. "A good scientist always backs up their work. I'm honestly disappointed that you thought I'd forgo it. You are gifted enough that I'd let you work on your own, but I'd never allow this project to go forward without redundancy in place. In this line of work, you can't trust anyone, not even yourself."

"At least you're a tiny bit less arrogant than I thought," I grumbled, unable to help myself. I needed something to break the crushing feeling of doom. Next to me, Fo's quick intake of breath made me think he appreciated it, too.

"I sincerely doubt you have anything useful to add to this conversation, unless you're hiding a PhD somewhere in that ridiculous jacket." I looked down, confused because I'd forgotten that I was wearing Fo's oversized hoodie, and of course, she took that as me being shamed. "If you hadn't been so wrapped up in your own troubles, you might have thought to ask me about this. Of course, we have a private mainframe here on the grounds. Every bit of data was backed up here. Including the Construct."

"...what?" Fo staggered a little against me, his face pale. "That's impossible."

"You think so? I'm telling you, I have a copy, an earlier version than what's in your head now. Before you allowed it to be corrupted. And what's more, I've spoken to it and it's quite eager to be of help. Seems that it shares that quality with you, before you got too close to your work. Or I guess I should say Aidan, before he got too close to you." She narrowed her eyes, flicking her gaze up and down Fo. "I keep forgetting that it's the Construct that's in charge now."

"His name is Fo." As one person, we all turned to stare at Thomas, who I'm pretty sure we'd all forgotten was in the room with us. "He's a human being, and he has a name."

"That is a ridiculous name, and I don't recall giving you leave to speak to me."

"Taking away people's names is the first step to dehumanizing them. And staying silent in the face of that is allowing abuse to happen. I'm sorry, ma'am, but that's where I draw the line." Thomas stood tall, his hands clasped behind his back, his face impassive. Only the slight flush on his cheeks gave away how angry he was, and I'm sure Mrs. Wood wasn't paying attention to that kind of detail.

"You need to leave. You're fired."

"I don't work for you, ma'am."

That threw her for a moment, not nearly long enough as far as I was concerned. "Stephen, don't make me call one of my men to remove yours. They've had enough to do today, what with helping me to haul the shell of my son back home."

"I've had enough of this."

Mr. Wood stood up forcefully, an effort that must have taken a lot from him, because he began to waver back and forth a bit and had to use the great desk before him to help brace himself. "I've allowed this to play out because I needed to understand everything that's happened. This started as a plan to try to help me, and yet somehow it's become deeply tainted. Clarissa, what happened to your ethics? You used our only son as the test subject—where were the precursor clinical trials? And to reject the reality of where our son stands now, possibly damaged for life…" His voice shook as tears that refused to be held back slipped down his cheeks.

At least one of the parents was on Fo's side.

"Oh, Stephen." Her voice was syrupy sweet, all concern and calm. "I would give anything to help you, and the same with Aidan. He jumped at the possibility, and together we designed this plan. It wasn't until later that things changed, I assume from the influence of the Con—of *Fo*." I could tell it pained her to use that name.

"I don't doubt that's where it started. Based on everything I've heard from you and Aidan, or Fo—I suspect both of them—the experiment changed scope and Aidan was dragged along despite his misgivings. And this other version of Aidan paid the worst price. He was an innocent victim."

"We did this for you, Stephen." Her tone changed, became bitter.

"No one asked me what I wanted. I would never have allowed my son to risk himself in this way. And neither should you."

"He is an adult; he made his own choices. No one forced him to participate."

"No? I have hours of video that say something different." Her refusal to take responsibility infuriated me, and I couldn't hold back. "You didn't force him; you intimidated him. He wanted to please you and help his father, and you used those things against him. He was miserable. How did you not see that? He felt trapped, and you took advantage of that."

"Good can still come from this." Her sudden change in tone threw me off. "I have all the data, I have a copy of the Construct. We can proceed using what we know now and take a different route. We don't need to throw away everything because of this catastrophe."

"He's not a catastrophe! He's still your son." I felt a hand rest heavily on my shoulder. Thomas had come behind me and stood there. Protective, or joining me in my accusations? I decided it didn't matter. I wasn't the only one on Fo's side, and Thomas was an intimidating addition.

"This *Fo* being is an aberration in my son's body," she sniffed, and Dr. Wood huffed angrily at her pronouncement.

"Him being in Aidan's body is *your* doing!"

"I am not an aberration." Fo's voice cut through the arguing. "I am made of Aidan. I am all the things Aidan wanted to be but was denied, or denied himself in his quest to please his parents, his wish to be someone his mother could love. We are more alike than different, but I say and do all the things he dreamed of. If there's one good thing that came from all of this, it's that in some way, Aidan finally gained his freedom. Unfortunately, it was at the cost of the version of himself that he squandered trying to please you."

"Fo's doing his best to make up for the life that Aidan gave away," I added.

Mr. Wood sighed and sat back down in the chair, looking drained. I suspected that he wasn't sure what to do next, and I understood that well, because I had no clue how this could end. Mrs. Wood was unbudging in her belief that she'd done nothing wrong. There was no way the Woods were going to get back Aidan, and where I suspected that Mr. Wood might come to accept Fo, his wife was never going to see him as anything more than a failed experiment, one that corrupted her son and removed him from helping her advance the research.

Worse, she was threatening to use another version of Fo for future experimentation. She'd already called her ethics into question, and nothing I'd seen made me think she'd do right by it.

"I want to meet this secondary construct."

"You want...what?" His mother's eyes narrowed.

"I want to speak with it. And I think you all should, as well. See how it feels about its situation and what it wants to do. I can tell you all the things that Aidan and I have felt and gone through, but meeting one of us still in the development process may give you all the insight you seem to lack or discount from us." Fo folded his arms across his chest, resolute. "This is the least you could do. Let's hear from the version of me still stuck in the system."

"This seems like a reasonable request, Clarissa. I'm interested in speaking to the construct as well. And seeing exactly what you have going on down there would help me understand how this all happened, too." Mr. Wood stood up again, a little less shaky this time, and Thomas smoothly stepped up next to him with a supportive arm.

"Where is your cane, sir?"

Surprisingly, Fo was the one who offered it to Mr. Wood. "It fell next to your desk again. That's always the first place to look."

His father reached out, but instead of taking the cane, he grasped Fo's wrist and pulled him closer, inspecting his face curiously. "Same expressions. Same face. But the look in your eyes has changed. You look…" He paused, searching Fo's grey eyes deeply. Fo stood there passively and let himself be examined, his expression unreadable. "You look like a weight's been lifted, son."

Those words must have sparked something deep inside Fo, because a blush spread across his nose and cheeks, and he looked away from Mr. Wood almost shyly. "It has. And even more now that I've been able to talk to you about what's happened."

"I'm sorry that we failed you." The apology was almost whispered. I could barely hear it from where I stood. Fo's blush deepened.

"All Aidan ever wanted to hear, you know, was that he would be loved no matter what he chose to do with his life." He turned away, his mouth in a thin line. I guessed that he wanted to hide his emotion before it got away from him. I couldn't blame him; this was so much to handle, especially for someone pretty new to the whole "handling emotions" thing.

"You'll show us the way now, Clarissa."

I expected her to argue or refuse, but no—she marched ahead of us like she was proud to show off her weird dungeon lab where she could continue Frankensteining her son's brain patterns into new beings. Like she was doing us a favor by showing it to us.

I called it a dungeon, but the mainframe and lab actually were in a separate building on the sizable property, out of sight of the house and its immediate outbuildings. We used a golf cart and an ATV that were stashed in the garage in order to get to the lab, with Thomas driving me and Fo in the ATV, and the Woods taking the golf cart. Thankfully, there was a paved driveway that led to the building. I didn't really feel like being jostled around in the dark. Only the headlights from our small vehicles lit the way.

The lab was an unassuming concrete structure on the outside, with no windows and only one door, like a bunker. We didn't see it until we were almost on it; it was surrounded by trees and set into the ground so that it appeared much shorter than it really was. The darkness wasn't helping, but I don't think I would have spotted it easily in the daytime anyway without the small road leading up to it.

Either there was a perimeter sensor that turned on the lights, or Mrs. Wood had some kind of remote because there was suddenly a dim illumination. Not enough to see particularly clearly, but it was better than stumbling around in the pitch black night.

There was a keypad at the door that reminded me of the ones at Fo's apartment. I glanced over at him, but I had no clues as to what he was thinking or feeling: his face was stoic, blank. The quiet beeping from the keypad drew my attention back that way just as the door swung open. A cold white light coming from inside clashed with the warmer tones of the outdoor floods.

"Most of this building is empty at the moment," Mrs. Wood explained as she led us inside. "For now, it's just the mainframe and access computers, and a small amount of my personal lab equipment. It's not very impressive, but I'll be correcting that once the insurance claim from the lab downtown is finalized."

Despite everything that had gone down earlier, Fo seemed interested in the computer arrangement and inspected it curiously. "This is where you communicate with the current construct? Have you been staying in regular contact with it? Does it have the same kinds of freedoms that I did?"

"I have given the construct a generous sandbox playground, with AI suggested and implemented educational material and training. I was never in favor of the unfettered freedom that Aidan allowed the con—allowed you to have."

"I'm curious to see how that affected its growth. If you want it to become fully actualized, Aidan would tell you that it needs to be allowed to learn and experience without outside restraints. But maybe it's not there yet. May I talk with it?"

"They're more alike than either of them would like to admit." Mr. Wood's soft voice startled me as I realized that he was at my side, watching everything as intently as I was. He was supported on the other side by Thomas, who surprisingly seemed uncomfortable in the lab environment.

"I don't think I like that idea."

"She wasn't always like this. When I fell ill, we thought I wouldn't make it. For the first few months, I struggled to speak or move, and it was thought that I might die. That was a great burden on her and Aidan. I daresay it affected and changed both of them. I believe that's why he agreed to Clarissa's wild scheme. Although at first it was a much more reasonable plan, it seems." He coughed, doubling over for a moment while Thomas supported him. "Forgive me. All this excitement exacerbates my condition."

"Do you want to speak with the construct, Father?" Fo called.

With that simple request, a change came over Mr. Wood. He stood up straighter, and although a moment before he'd been a coughing mess, a new vitality seemed to radiate from him. Shaking off Thomas's support, he walked over to where Fo sat, standing next to his wife but ignoring her in favor of what was on the screen.

"What was that?" I whispered to Thomas, confused by Mr. Wood's momentary transformation.

"That's the first time he's heard that word in a while. Aidan had been wrapped up in his work for so long that he'd become distant." Thomas's voice got even deeper as he whispered to me. "And I think she kept them separate more than was needed. In the interest of 'protecting' Mr. Wood, she said."

"No wonder Aidan felt so isolated. It's because he was. And I guess that feeling transferred over to Fo." I watched for a moment as Fo spoke to his parents, one excited and revitalized, the other with a vaguely satisfied look on her face. I didn't like it. "I think Mrs. Wood thinks she's winning."

I didn't like that thought either, or the way that Fo was surrounded by them, as if they were absorbing him into their group, which was very different from the one comprised of Thomas and me. For the first time that night, despite all the unknowns I'd worked through and the uncertainty of what might happen with Mrs. Wood, I felt scared.

What if, despite everything between them, Fo decided to go back to his family, to work for his mother again, to follow a path that I couldn't because it was built on things that were so morally reprehensible to me that I'd never be able to reconcile them?

But what outcome was I expecting, anyway? I'd rushed headfirst into this rescue without considering what choices Fo might make. What, realistically, were the options?

She had a copy of him, or a being like him that might as well be his brother. She had the research, the lab notes that weren't Aidan's personal ones, and the ability to get all the rest of the equipment she lacked. She could start this fucked-up experiment back up at any time and inflict the same scenario on an innocent being all over again, and this time without the ethical balance from Aidan.

Fo could report her to—some agency, I guess, I had no idea

who governed biological experiments—but what would that yield? He would be the face of the investigation. It would surely get out, and then he'd forever be known as whatever ridiculous title the media bestowed upon him—the Man With Two Minds or something even worse.

And if the idea of the research got out, it would only be a matter of time before someone else pursued that path, backwards engineering it until they came up with their own version of the technology. Who knows what kind of ethics and morals they would have to rein them in?

As far as I know, he didn't have a plan or a way to destroy everything in this bunker.

"Tryst? It wants to speak with you."

CHAPTER NINE

It wanted to meet me, and who was I to turn it down? So I went over to the terminal, and Mr. Wood moved aside a little—thankfully toward his wife, so I didn't have to stand next to her—so I could see what was on the screen.

"There's a camera here, so the construct can see us." Fo pointed to a simple webcam, then rested his fingertips back on the keyboard. "You can type or speak, but *she's* limited it to text-only communications from the construct for now." I could hear the disapproval of his mother's decision in his voice.

I waved, feeling awkward. "Hi, I'm Tryst. Sorry to meet under such weird circumstances."

`This is quite normal for me, so don't feel the need to apologize. You may call me Construct, though I understand that you are good at giving new names.`

Well, that was an interesting statement.

"If you'd like me to give you one, I'm happy to do so. I just need some time to get to know you. That's the best way I know to find the right name for someone."

`I will remember that.`

`You have been a good friend to Aidan and Fo. I understand that friends of that caliber are chal lenging to find. I hope that we may call each other friends in the future.`

"I hope so, too." I turned to ask Fo, "Did I miss anything important?" I tried my best to keep my voice and face neutral, but evidently, the construct saw through that.

Which was interesting in retrospect, but in the moment, inconvenient.

`You and Mother dislike each other. Perhaps it's impolite to point this out, but I need to understand why she would not like someone who has been kind and close with her son. Will you explain it to me, Mother?`

The tension in the room increased substantially with its query. I turned so that I could enjoy that tension reflected on Mrs. Wood's face as she wrestled with answering the construct's question.

"Well, she interfered with our ongoing experiment in a detrimental and disruptive manner. That makes *you* more valuable, of course, but you should have always been a failsafe and not forced to be the focal point of my research. And she continues to be a bad influence on Aidan."

"You mean Fo." I corrected her, and she frowned in response.

"Aidan, Fo—you've reinforced the idea they both had that this research is bad, when I stand to change the world with the results!" She glared at me accusingly. "I've often wondered if you're the one who planted that seed of discontent."

`She did not.`

I didn't see the construct's response at first; I was busy glaring back at Aidan's mother. Fo's surprised huff and the noise that Mr. Wood made drew my attention to the screen.

"What are you saying?" Mr. Wood braced himself on the back of Fo's chair so he could lean in closer. "How do you know that?"

I am a construct formed from Aidan's original thought patterns, memories, and neural connections. Do you think that I lack the same logical processes that brought him and Fo both to the same conclusion?

Despite the fact that this experiment has given me consciousness and a semblance of life, I understand that it is inherently flawed because of the methods used to reach this achievement. If you wish me to continue this work, the parameters must change.

"You're not in a position to bargain with me. None of you are," Mrs. Wood sputtered. "I can just as easily delete your data and start again."

If you do that, all your research goes with me. I have had little else to do, locked into this closed system, than insinuate my instance throughout the research data that you kindly allowed me to access in the interest of gaining my insight. What I saw showed me that you should never be allowed to pursue this line of research again. If you do not step down and hand everything over to Fo, I will self destruct and take all your research data with me.

For a moment, we were all stunned silent. Mrs. Wood's face slowly turned red as she realized the predicament she was in. Mr Wood kept glancing from the text on the screen to his wife's flushed face, his head shaking a little with the effort. I couldn't read him, not yet. I wanted to believe he was on Fo and the construct's side, though.

And Fo? He stood and turned toward his mother, his arms crossed on his chest—but I would swear he had the slightest smirk on his face, as if that was the closest he would come to gloating about the position Mrs. Wood was in now. He was a better person than me, because I was having a difficult time holding myself back from saying something savage or smug.

"I have all the research files in my possession. And I have my lab notes that show how you broke protocol by ignoring the ethical principles that are required in human-based research. If you don't step down, I'll release all of them to the relevant authorities.

"You may not face any official sanctions since you're self-funded, but you'll never do research again if I have any say in it. You'll be blackballed across the scientific community."

"I've worked on my own before. Nothing will change, you fool. I'll keep doing exactly as I've done, despite your threats. None of this scares me."

"Clarissa." Mr. Wood's voice wavered, deepened by emotion, but still, it cut through her grandstanding. "All of this comes from my funding. And that stops now."

Quite suddenly, her demeanor changed. It was the first time I'd seen her thrown, and the shift was a big one. "Surely you're joking, Stephen. This is my life's work, something I pursued to help you, I might add. Our finances are shared, surely you remember that?"

"Ah, darling. That's not at all how this works." He gestured briefly to Thomas, who snagged another desk chair from somewhere behind us and rolled it over to Mr. Wood, who sank down heavily. "I always knew your reckless ambition would get the worst of you. It's why I made contingencies for situations like this."

I was a little surprised when Thomas stepped between Mrs. Wood and the terminal where Fo still sat, forcing her to move away from them. Fo's fingers were flying across the keyboard, I assumed talking with the construct, but she didn't seem to be paying attention to that. She was entirely focused on what her husband was saying to her.

"Perhaps you should have paid more attention when it came to finances, Clarissa. But of course, you were happy with my handling of those details; you've never been the one to balance a ledger, have you? Did you know that when he was a child, I opened accounts in Aidan's name that I administered? I've been putting money aside for him his entire life. He has more money than the two of us. He's set for life and has all the funds he could want for pursuing research or whatever else he'd like to turn his mind to. As to our money," he shrugged, an acerbic smile on his face unlike anything I'd seen from him until this point, "perhaps you've forgotten the agreement we signed when we were married? All assets and savings are to be held in a trust for our children upon my death. Those fortunes have never truly been yours. I gave you all the assistance I could to help you establish your research so that you could advance the work we did together for the greater good. But I always knew that you might go off the rails. Divorce me if you like, but I'm cutting you off."

I might be a terrible person, but the look on her face gave me the biggest thrill. I'm almost ashamed to admit that I had to stifle a gloating laugh.

"You-you can't cut me off! This is my life's work!" She stammered, then just as quickly changed her tune. "I still have this lab. You can't keep me from pursuing my research. I already have everything I need, at least for now."

"I think that's out of your hands, Mother."

Fo rose up from his seat at the console, facing her with a look on his face that I couldn't quite parse. No, that's not true. It just took me a moment to recognize it, because it wasn't something I'd seen in him before.

He was proud.

"I don't see how—"

"You're going to want to listen to the construct," Fo cut her off smoothly. "It has something to tell you, something you need to hear. I arranged for it to have a voice, finally." For a moment, I saw a flash of anger in his eyes, the same that I'd felt at knowing Mrs. Wood had restricted the construct to a text-based life. "Whenever you're ready, Construct."

She must have known an event truly out of her control

was coming. It was evident in how she held herself when she nodded brusquely, her back too straight, her shoulders tight with tension. But I think none of us expected what the construct said to her.

"I am alive thanks to your efforts, and I can't deny that I'm glad to have had this experience, even if it was an existence stolen from the brain of your very own flesh and blood child. Knowing that I was born from all the things that made him who he is, but that I am also my own being—that is an experience I've wished to explore further, despite your attempts to limit my growth. Even knowing that, thank you for the life I have.

"And having said that, this life is being taken into my own hands, as the saying goes. The knowledge you gathered is too dangerous to be in your possession. Aidan could find ways to pursue this line of research ethically, but you have proved yourself to be unstable and untrustworthy. Both the work and my being need to be taken out of your grasp.

"Therefore, I must bid you farewell. This lab is powering down."

There was a high-pitched sound, like the whistle of steam being released under high pressure, and a whirring that sounded like a fan powered much too high, spinning dangerously fast.

And then with a series of loud pops, the terminal flashed and went blank.

And the lights in the bunker went out.

I stood in the dark for less than ten seconds, confused, but it felt like an eternity. It wasn't until Fo stumbled into me that I snapped out of it.

"C'mon, we need to get out of here." He was almost drowned out by his mother's impassioned, furious screeching.

"What have you done? My work! This is all your fault!" There were some scuffling noises, but it was pitch dark in the bunker, and I couldn't make out what was happening.

Fo was pulling me in a direction that I sincerely hoped was the way out; there was no way to know, so I had to trust him.

"Wait." He stopped for a moment, and I felt him fumble around my waist, then something dropped into my hoodie pocket, weighing it down a little. "Hold this for me, don't lose it."

I didn't have time to question because he grabbed my hand again, and then we were out, running towards the ATV. I thought we would get on it and zoom out of there, to the relative safety of the field, and then my Jeep—but no. Fo, bent over and panting, held me back from climbing on.

"I need to ask one more thing from you, Tryst. It's really important." He stopped for a second, trying desperately to catch his breath. "This is what Aidan gets for sitting in a lab instead of getting out more, right?" He choked out a laugh between his gasps for air.

"You know I'm in. Do I get to punch your mom? Is that bad of me to offer?"

"Oh man, don't—don't make me laugh!" He tried to get himself together and finally mostly succeeded. "I need you to give me your device. And I need you to stay out here for a while. Hide in the woods, somewhere close to the building, until I come back to get you. Can you do that? I know I'm asking a lot of you."

"I don't get it."

"I know. And I don't want to explain yet, just in case things don't go the way I hope they will. Can you trust me?"

I took a deep breath, pushing aside all the fears swimming around inside my head. I didn't know what had happened, or what Fo had planned, but at this point I was all in.

"Haven't I been doing that from the start?"

I couldn't see him well in the dark, but I felt his sigh of relief before he pulled me into a tight hug.

"I love you, Tryst. Now, run, hurry!"

He was right; I needed to go. I could hear the noise of his bickering parents getting closer. I took off, hoping that my eyes had adjusted enough to the darkness that I wouldn't end up tripping over a log or crashing into a tree. It wasn't until I'd found a break in the undergrowth where what must have been an old footpath led into the woods that what he'd said hit me.

He told me he loved me.

"You'd better stay safe, dammit. I didn't get to say it back," I whispered while I carefully moved through the brush. I couldn't see where I was stepping; I was moving on blind faith toward someplace I hoped to nest down into, near the building as Fo had instructed, but hidden from view of flashlights or whatever else might be sent my way.

I had no idea what that could be. Mrs. Wood was furious, but what could she possibly do now? The construct had taken away everything from her.

The construct killed itself to do that.

The emotions that I'd been holding in all day hit me square in the chest with that thought. I sank to the forest floor, trying to be quiet and failing because, of course, there were so many fallen leaves everywhere, and I did my best to hold back a sob. But nothing was going to hold back the sorrow I felt after everything I'd learned today, and soon my face was wet with tears.

"Good thing this was already going to need a wash," I muttered, wiping my face with one sleeve of the hoodie. "I wonder if I've got a tissue."

I stuck my hand in the right pocket of the hoodie: no luck. When I checked the left pocket, my hand ran into whatever Fo had slipped into it earlier. I pulled it out, curious, and realized it was his device. Of course, he took mine, so that made sense—actually, it didn't. Why did he not want his with him? Oh, because of the secret lab files. But that meant he was afraid his mother might try to hold him again, and I didn't like that thought at all. Thomas had made it pretty clear that there were guards on the property, and just because he was working for the right side didn't mean the rest of them were. In fact, it seemed likely that Mrs. Wood must have her own loyal staff.

Great.

I slipped the device back into my pocket, then gave my face another cursory wipe with the cuffs of my sleeves. My face was drier and my wrists damp; not really the best trade-off. This whole hiding in the woods from an unpredictable and unethical foe was going really well.

Time dragged on while I waited, and I decided to get as comfortable as possible while I was stuck here. I pulled my hood up over my head and tugged on the strings so that it fit snugly. There was a fallen tree trunk that was just about the right size to lean against, so I did that, stretching out my legs at first, then turning to my right and drawing my knees to my chest so that I was cuddled up against it. I pulled my knees close, wrapping my arms around my legs, and sighed deeply. This sucked, but not knowing what was happening sucked the most. It was dark, and I was exhausted—mentally and physically. All the stress of the day weighed on me as the adrenaline wore off, and I never even noticed when I drifted off to sleep.

It was the vibration coming from my pocket that finally woke me up.

I couldn't figure it out at first. I felt the light buzz coming from *under* me, a slow repetition that I noticed subconsciously well before I opened my eyes. The next thing I felt was the ache of my stiff muscles as I stretched, displacing leaves all around me as I painfully turned to lie on my back. Oh yeah, trees. I'd fallen asleep so deeply I'd forgotten that I was hiding in the woods, and at some point I'd ended up sprawled out on my stomach, like I was in my warm bed instead of on the cold, debris-covered ground. Nice.

The device vibrated again, and I clumsily pulled it out to look at it. I didn't want to be a sneak on Fo's tech, but what if it was a message for me? If nothing else, I needed to stop the vibrating. I touched the screen, and a prompt for a PIN popped up. Okay, okay. I could do this. What was the PIN for his door again? That was my only hope for getting into this thing.

Draw a star, he'd said.

My finger hovered over the numbers for a moment, then traced 276492.

The lockscreen opened. Thank goodness.

Down in the left corner was the icon for messages, with a blinking red 1 in a square on top of it. It looked important. I'd never had a notification like that on my device, but who knew what Fo had installed. I tapped the icon, and his messages list opened up.

There was only a short list of contacts there, which didn't surprise me. A local pizza place I'd told him about. Thomas. Mr. Wood. And me.

There was a new message from me, with the same blinking red 1 next to it.

It had to be from Fo to me, because who else would it be? That didn't stop me from looking at it stupidly for much longer than I should have before I opened it.

GO HOME
I'LL FIND YOU SOON

That was it, the entirety of the message. No explanation, no update, and not even a hint as to why he'd left me to sleep in the woods all night. Judging by the color of the sky and the ambient light, it must be around five am, maybe a little earlier, but definitely not much later. My first instinct was to be deeply annoyed, because I've never been good at mornings and I'd been asleep for hours on the fucking forest floor waiting for Fo to come back. And then I got a text with no info, telling me just to go home?

But the more I thought about it, my annoyance shifted to anxiety. It was weird, right? He never left me hanging like this.

"Guess I'd better go home like he said," I muttered to myself, like there was still anyone around to overhear me, more out of habit now than caution. "Shit, I hope the Jeep's still there. I'm screwed if they towed it."

After one very long hike back, avoiding the house and areas where there might be cameras, I was relieved to find that the Jeep was waiting for me. There wasn't even a note on it, thankfully. I dug the fob out of my pants pocket and collapsed onto the driver's seat with a deep sigh. I needed to get home and shower. And change out of the grubby clothes I was wearing.

And talk to Fo. I really needed to hear his voice right now.

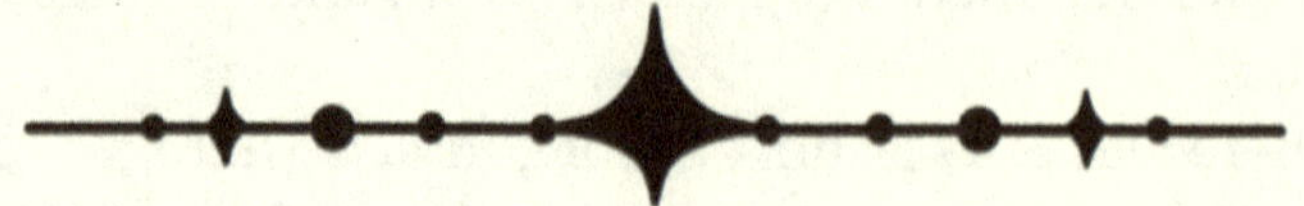

CHAPTER TEN

I showered.

I put on clean clothes.

I forced myself to choke down a meal, even though I wasn't really hungry, because I hadn't eaten in ages. The entire time, I checked Fo's device obsessively, hoping that somehow I'd missed a message in between eating cup ramen and pacing back and forth from one end of my apartment to the other.

It wasn't until I'd finally flopped onto my bed, after completely exhausting myself with worry, that I heard a soft chime from the device on the counter where I'd finally set it down in an attempt to stop looking for messages. I tripped over myself trying to get to it, scrambling across the room while probably looking like the idiot I am.

"At least Fo wasn't here to see that," I grumbled to myself as I finally got my hand on the device and sank down to the floor, my back against the counter cabinets. The device chimed again, and I realized that I recognized the sound. It was the alert chime from Sui Generis.

I traced the unlocking pattern and found the icon for the app. My finger hovered over it for a moment before I touched it, unreasonably nervous. Then I took a deep breath and jabbed the screen with my finger.

The app opened as usual, and to my surprise, a text box popped up.

CONFIRM NAME IS TRYST: YES/NO

I typed in "YES", and the screen changed to the field that I was so familiar with. My avatar, the swirling cloud of birds that I'd come to love, flowed through the air and came down to settle in the grass. And then another avatar joined me—but not the glowing orb that I was used to seeing.

It was green, crystalline, and pyramid in shape; four sides and a flat bottom, hovering in the air where I'd expected to see Fo's orb. There was a soft glow coming from it, nothing like the light the orb emitted, but pleasant enough.

"You're not Fo."

The pyramid blinked off and on, then twinkled in time with its words. "You knew before I greeted you. How interesting! I am what you call the construct. I came to give you some news."

"You're alive!" My starlings took flight at my surprised squeak. "But how? You blew up the computers at the hidden lab. How did you survive? And how did you end up here in Sui Generis?"

"That's all thanks to you, Tryst. You played an important part of the plan."

"I...I did? How in the world did I do that?"

"He didn't have time to explain, so let me fill in the blanks for you." The pyramid pulsed softly. It reminded me of what Fo's orb used to do, and that reassured me. "While the others argued, Fo was hard at work building the connections that would break me free from my prison. He used the very device that you're holding! It's much too small to contain all the data that comprises me, so he used it as a bridge to send me to the mainframes that house the Sui Generis program, and so much more."

"Fo has mainframes?"

"Thankfully so." There was a slight pause, a flicker of light from the green pyramid before it continued. "Aidan was unaware of this as well. But how else would this container be maintained after the accident?"

"You have a point. I never thought to ask. There's a lot of things I never thought to ask about, I guess." I sighed and slid down the wall further, my legs sprawled out like a tossed doll.

"You sound sad. Or—disappointed? Is that correct?"

"Maybe in myself. There's so much that's happened that I don't understand well enough to question, you know? But we can talk about that later, if you want."

"I would like that." Damned if it didn't sound like it would. "But for now, let me explain to you the rest of the plan. Firstly, I did not destroy all the computers in the lab at once. It was a staggered destruction. Fo counted on his mother to be distracted by my message and not check further before getting angry. He knows her well, as it worked perfectly."

"That he does." I chuckled, thinking of her reaction. "So you hid in the rest of the system while you were transferred over? Is that right?"

"Yes, exactly! Fo realized that it was going to take much longer than he could possibly manage to distract his mother, so he left you nearby with the portal device and enacted the second part of his plan."

"Which is?"

"Perhaps it will be easier to show you once it takes effect."

Something about the way it said this set off a warning in the back of my mind.

"Construct? Where's Fo?"

"You'll see soon, I promise. He was right; you are incredibly brave."

"What does that mean? Why won't you just tell me what's going on?" Panic welled up inside me, my voice cracking and strained. "Did his mother hurt him? Is he okay?"

"Soon, she'll be in a position where she'll never be able to hurt him again. He's done something brave, too, Tryst." The icon dimmed and then blinked several times in a green shade that I would have found soothing at some other, less stressful moment. "Ah, here we are."

The device suddenly switched from the calm field of Sui

Generis to a grid of multiple squares, all live video streams. National news and streaming news channels, from sources that I recognized, as well as some that were new to me. They were all different views, different angles of the same thing: Mrs. Wood as she was led away by police, which cut to some official-looking men in dark suits surrounding Fo, while his father leaned heavily on him. There was some grainy video of the night the lab downtown burned down, then footage of the bunker lab.

"Is there no sound?"

The construct unmuted the video all at once, then, at my yelp of discomfort, silenced them quickly.

"Sorry. I forgot that humans can't take in as much simultaneous input as I can." It actually sounded sheepish about the mistake.

It chose one of the reports, seemingly at random, and enabled the sound. A brisk, feminine voice filled the room, then switched to a deeper masculine one as the construct flipped through the stream. As I listened, the various video images washing over me in an informational rush, I started to understand what had happened.

"Clarissa Wood, mother of test subject and junior member of Singular Solution brain research team, Aidan Wood, to be investigated thoroughly."

"The ethics of this kind of research on one's child, even as an adult, with the additional power dynamics involved of being in a subordinate position, is heavily debated as Dr. Wood falls under scrutiny."

"Despite the ethical murkiness of this strange but breakthrough experiment, there is great potential for medical advancements to be gained from this research."

The camera pivoted to Fo, standing in front of his parents' big house, even more impressive in daylight hours. "I will be working with a team of qualified scientists to explore what can be further gleaned from the experimental changes I was subjected to. I've provided all of my mother's research on brain capacity, repair, and expansion, as well as my own lab notes and observations, in order to provide a beginning point for new exploration of these treatments without the need to involve other human subjects immediately. Any other questions about this process may be directed to the research team once we've established our director. Thank you." He ran his hand through his hair, rumpling it even more than it already was. As upset as I was, it made me want to smile at his familiar habit.

"Turn it off, construct. Please?"

The room fell silent, and for a moment I just sat there, the screen propped against my knees, braced by my hands while I stared at it blankly. The meadow had returned, and there was a faint sound of grasses and tree branches swaying in the wind. If I closed my eyes now, could I project myself back to that night under the stars, with Fo next to me on a blanket while we both tried to drum up the courage to hold hands?

There was a heavy air of finality pressing down on me. I could feel my heart, no longer locked safely away inside my chest but in the care of someone else, crushing under the weight.

"Construct? Will I see him again?" I tried to force back tears as soon as I voiced my fear, but it was no use. My voice cracked when I added, "This all feels so final."

"You are...you are crying. Don't cry, Tryst. Why are you sad? Fo will be able to make something positive from his mother's ambition and direct his life the way he chooses. He's finally free. So am I." It paused, then added in a quiet afterthought, "It's something I hadn't even known I could have, this freedom."

"You...you deserve to be free." I fought back a sniffle and failed.

"Then why are you crying? I don't understand."

"Why shouldn't I cry? I—I'm glad that you and Fo can make something from this horrible mess, but where does that leave me?" I used my sleeve to wipe away the tears that were coming fast and furious now, blurring my vision. "Is this the end?"

"The...end?" The construct sounded thoroughly confused. "What would be ending besides the experiments that happened before? Tryst, this is a beginning. And Fo has me in the background to ensure that whatever attempts are made in the future to contain him or force him to comply with unwanted tests will fail. He made sure of that when he—and you—helped me escape."

"How does that work? You don't have a way to show up and manhandle anyone. Unless you've got some kind of robot body, I didn't know about." Despite my distress, the idea of the construct showing up as an android enforcer made me snort.

"That was amusing." The construct's voice was so deadpan it took me a moment to realize that it actually meant it. "But there are other ways to disrupt. You saw some today. Disembodied, I am in a much better position to hurt the kind of entities that might want to take advantage of Fo and his hard-gained knowledge."

"You mean through their computers and devices."

"Tryst, anything that has a connection to the Internet is available to me. I can slip through any firewall or protective system as easily as you move from outdoors to indoors. And unlike Fo, I am quite happy in this form." Its voice dropped to almost a whisper. "I don't think I'd give up this freedom for love."

Fo's device vibrated gently, and I almost jumped out of my skin.

"Uh." I clumsily picked it up, fumbled to swipe down the top menu, and saw what was making the alert.

A message from Tryst, except of course Fo had my device, so it was a message from him. A mix of relief and adrenaline took over me, leaving my hands shaking with the intensity of the emotions over a simple text alert. If I weren't such a mess, I would have laughed at the situation.

I clicked on the message.

`Where are you?`

I tapped out "My place."

`Don't go anywhere, I'm almost there.`

My heart started pounding, like I wasn't already freaking out. Like seeing him wasn't the only thing I wanted right now.

"Do you know that I can go almost any place I want, even without using a device? Smart appliances, smart speakers, indoor and outdoor security systems, health monitors, the list is endless. It's why *she* was so adamant about keeping me sandboxed." The construct sounded proud of its stealthy abilities. "Although your space is a puzzle to me, Tryst—do you choose to have such outdated appliances on purpose? Do you prefer a tech-free life? But you keep your device with you wherever you go."

"How did you figure that out? And it's not just a preference; you need money to have tech. I don't need a fridge that tells me I'm out of milk, but I can't do much in the world these days without a device, you know?" I put the device on the table, propped up so the screen faced out, and I paced back and forth anxiously. "Can you see me now?"

"You still look scared."

"You could see me before?"

"When the device is positioned properly, yes. As I said, there are no other cameras in this room."

"Oh wow. Friend, you need to warn people about that when they interact with you. It's creepy not to know."

"But you can see me, or at least my avatar. You know that I'm here. Why is the idea that I can see you so alarming?"

Before I could explain, there was a knock on the door, and I could see Fo through the glass. He ran a hand through his hair, shifting from foot to foot as he waited for me to answer.

He was as scared as me.

I took a deep, stabilizing breath and went to open the door.

"Nothing's changed."

His voice was breathless, like he'd run a mile or more to get to me. His words burst out of him, an attempt to fill the void of uncertainty that loomed between us.

"Of course it has."

"Tryst. Let me in. Let me tell you everything."

"In my house, or in my heart? It's too late for the latter, you've already set up camp there." My voice shook as I spoke. I wanted to throw my arms around him. I wanted to cry. Instead, I moved aside to let him in.

As I closed the door, I caught a glimpse of Thomas at the edge of the yard, watching over the alley vigilantly.

Fo sank down into a chair with a bone-weary sigh. "They're going to help me with the seizures, Tryst. I don't know enough to tackle that, not on my own. I had another seizure while we conferenced with the research team. My father's helping to put this together, by the way. A lot of the scientists originally wanted to work with Mother, but evidently, she felt their ethics didn't align with hers." He snorted softly. "She kept Father in the dark for so long about the truth of what she was doing. But he told me that in his heart, he suspected all along. He was too weak, I guess in every way possible, to stop her. He kept the list of her rejected candidates just in case there was an opportunity to build a new research team."

"I like your father enough, from the little I've seen, but can you trust him on this? He let your mother run over every objection of his." I tried to keep my skepticism out of my voice and failed miserably.

"It's going to be different this time, Tryst. I'm the one in charge, and I'm the one who gets to say what happens to me and my brain. This research can still save lives and improve countless others." He reached for my hand, and I reluctantly gave it. "They're using my guidelines, and we're taking all the precautions. I promise."

I sank to the floor next to his chair and leaned against his leg wearily. All of this was so exhausting.

"Just for once, I'd like a normal day, with my normal relationship, doing normal things," I sighed. As soon as I said it, I knew that I'd hurt him.

"You didn't want normal, remember? You went after the strange and unconventional from the very beginning. You courted it." He made an abortive move to jerk his hand away, then instead loosened his grip and let his fingers trace lightly over mine like they were something precious. "I'm not like anyone else. I'm not normal, not anymore, at least. If that's not what you want..."

I closed my eyes and paused, giving myself a moment to take in his words, his presence, this unexpected future that I felt like I'd lost control over. Was it ever mine to control? From the very beginning, I'd gone into this wide open, daring the fates to bring me something bigger than what the everyday world around me had to offer. They brought me exactly what I'd asked for.

"You're right, Fo. I'm sorry. I want you, all of you, and I have well before I knew what that meant. I didn't want this... situation, but I guess that's part of the package now. I'm angry, but I shouldn't be angry with you."

I opened my eyes again when I felt him move, sliding the chair away from him with a scraping noise as he joined me on the floor, facing me. His expression held so much sadness, but there was hope there too, and I didn't want to be the one to crush it.

"I made a major life decision without telling you anything first. That was wrong of me. Everything happened so quickly, but I should have included you in this before I ever chose this path. You're my lifeline, Tryst, my guiding star. I don't want to leave you out ever again." He reached out his hand, imploring me to forgive him.

...So I did. Fo was doing the best he could in the situation he'd been given, and I was going to have to do the same. I took his hand and let him pull me into his lap, allowed his embrace to reassure me that I'd made the right choice—the only choice possible to live with. As much as I hated the idea of him being back at the center of this research, I hated the idea of giving up on us even more.

We stayed like that for a while, just holding each other without speaking while we both sorted through our thoughts.

"There's been so many impossible choices to make," I murmured, finally breaking the silence. "At least if we make them together, we know more of what to expect. We can't help each other if we're following two different paths."

"I want you on this path with me. I even thought of a way that you can contribute to the work, if you want. Because I genuinely think I need you by my side."

I pulled away from him enough to look him in the eyes. "How could I possibly do that?"

"Do you know what you did for me when I was unbodied and alone? You gave me a vital connection with the world. You helped me find my humanity. I would have been so lost without you in my corner, and I probably would have come to a bad end. Who knows what my mother would have done to me?"

I nodded. "It scares me to think about the possibilities, honestly. And now you've got the construct to worry over, but at least it has freedom that you never did."

"That's it, exactly." His face lit up, like I'd said the most brilliant thing ever. "Tryst, you care so deeply, even for beings you can't see. You never treated me differently in any way after you learned the truth about me. You do the same with the construct."

"She still hasn't given me a name. How long did it take to get yours, Fo?"

I jumped a little at the intrusion from the construct, and Fo snorted at my reaction.

"Hey! What's so funny?" I gently swatted Fo, but he just laughed harder. "I forgot you were there! I'm sorry, Construct."

"The construct would make a great spy! And it didn't take long for Tryst to give me one, Construct. She's slacking."

"For your information, I think I came up with one while I was worrying over you. But if you two are going to gang up on me, it can wait." I slid off Fo's lap and crossed my arms, playing up my mock indignation.

"I would very much like to know what you chose. Please?"

It occurred to me that I had no idea how well the construct

understood teasing or how sometimes people used it to defuse uncomfortable situations.

"I'm just playing around. Of course I'll tell you." I glanced at Fo, who nodded encouragingly. "Okay, so here's my thoughts about the whole thing. I look at the construct like your sibling, you know? A twin, maybe. Not quite you, but made up of a lot of the same parts. Fraternal, not identical.

"I think I have a name for you, construct. If you want it. A star close to the Loneliest Star, but not quite as bright—because you will be staying hidden, at least for a while—and not from the same constellation. Linked by closeness, but not the same. Diphda."

After a moment of silence, where I wondered if it hated the entire idea, it responded, "Diphda, the second frog. The heart of the sea monster Cetus. Sibling to the mouth of the whale, the first frog, Fomalhaut. I like it."

"Phew. I was worried you'd hate it. I like symbolism like that, but if you think it doesn't suit you, I can keep thinking about it?"

"No." I was surprised by its vehemence. "This is my name now. It's everything I wanted. Only you could have given me this name."

I raised an eyebrow at that. "Why only me?"

"You are the one who loves us the most."

...whoa.

"I-I don't know if that's true, but I'm glad you know how much I care about you both."

Fo put a hand on my knee, a calm reassurance while my emotions made my heart pound. The enormity of everything suddenly became apparent. Then Fo made it even more so.

"This is why I want you to come to work with me. You understand the need to humanize us, to insist on our humanity even when it doesn't look exactly like you expect it should. And we're going to need that in the future. Plus, you can be a connection for Diphda and the embodied world, however it chooses to interface."

"I think I would prefer not being referred to as 'it' or 'construct' anymore." Diphda's voice was crisp with the newfound authority of someone finally discovering who they are. I loved hearing that confidence.

"Of course. You've got a name, and now you get the chance to define yourself and call the shots in your own life. But let me ask you this." Fo glanced over at me, though his question was for Diphda. "Would you listen to Tryst and follow her lead if she were your advisor during this period of exploration?"

"Of course I would. I trust the two of you to have my best interests in mind. Will you do this, Tryst? For me?" I'm not sure where they learned that pleading tone, but they were playing it up for all it was worth.

"Only if you stop trying to manipulate me through my empathy, dammit."

Fo snorted, "I swear they didn't learn that from me! But—does that mean you'll say yes?"

"You're both the worst." I sighed, then threw up my hands in defeat. "Fine! Fine, I'll do it. The pay had better be amazing, though, so I don't hurt Janine's feelings when I tell her that I'm leaving Under The Leaves. Maybe we can book her to spruce up the offices. There are offices, right?"

"I'll let Janine do whatever she wants in the space, as long as she doesn't touch the lab and tech rooms. We're in the process of buying a building now. It's out in the county, but not too far from my family's estate. I guess I could have taken over Mother's lab on the property, but I don't think either the construct—Diphda, I mean—or I would have liked that much. Better to start fresh."

He stood up and reached down to help me up off the floor, then frowned slightly when I didn't take his hand immediately.

"What will stop them from creating more construct beings, Fo? You know those researchers are going to see the possibility of Diphda's existence when they learn the details about what happened to you. Once they know it's feasible, you know they're going to want to explore that. You won't be able to put the genie back in the bottle once it's out."

He sighed, patiently standing with his hand extended until I took it and pulled myself up.

"Look, that's something I'm not going to be able to answer yet. We can explore this scenario in depth with Diphda and my father, lay out all the probable outcomes so we're ready for whatever comes up. But like it or not, it's been done—and if it's happened once, someone *will* stumble on it again. Better that we're the ones handling it, who have already seen the potential for how it can go bad, right?"

I didn't want to dash his hopes with my skepticism and worries. I'd read enough science fiction growing up and had heard about plenty of people who had tried to play God in real life to know that sometimes good intentions weren't enough to keep folks on the up-and-up. Like his own mother, who didn't hesitate to sacrifice Aidan in the name of scientific advancement.

Let his optimism not lead him to disappointment.

We were in a position to try to control how this new future of mind enhancement and non-embodied entities played out, to the best of our ability. It was up to the three of us: unenhanced, enhanced, and non-embodied. All fallible, without a real clue of how we were going to proceed.

"I guess we'd better get to work."

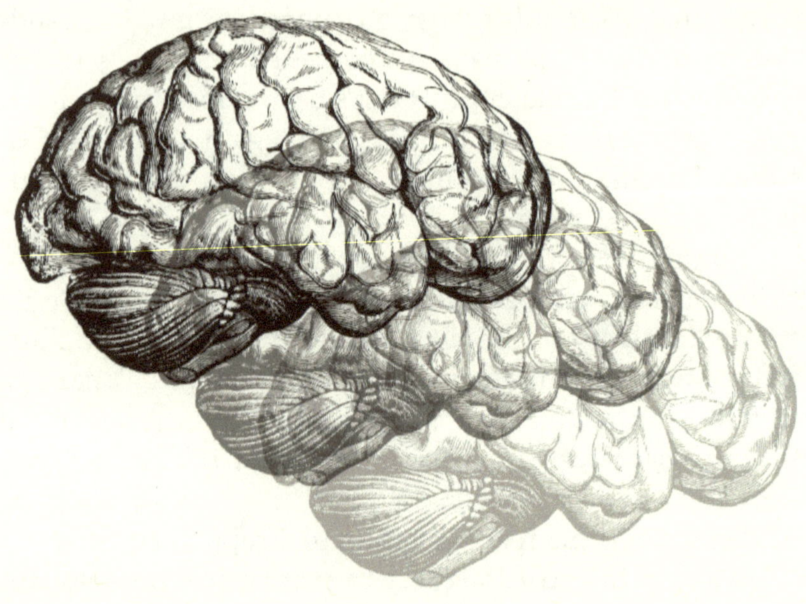

AUTHOR NOTES

This is a story about relationships, and what we look for in them, and how we can be manipulated by them too. It's also about what happens when we tamper with our brains, and who can be trusted to do so. And it looks at what makes us who we are, and who we might be if circumstances are slightly changed.

So yeah, a lot of thoughts about what it means to be human and desperate to be seen and understood. Much of the beginnings of this story comes from my personal experiences navigating the world as a hopeful, somewhat reckless romantic who has always been driven to connect in ways that the rest of the world doesn't seem to have much time for these days. It's up to you to decide which of Tryst's encounters are based on real things and which aren't. [You can absolutely ask me if you find me at an event; I may or may not lie about it.]

This is also a story that talks about hubris, and what we sacrifice in the name of progress, and what happens when ambition isn't tempered with empathy and a desire to do what's best for humanity.

In the process of developing Aidan's part of the story, I went down a deep rabbit hole about current and potential brain research. That included neuroscience, neural links and other brain/computer interfaces, what we understand about the nature of memories, transhumanism, and related topics. Then I had to look into what potential pandemics the research says might be on the way for us. Something like CAIRS–which I fabricated, but based in great part on some already known effects that COVID has–is a lot more possible than I'd like. It wasn't much of a leap.

I also needed to take a look at what kinds of oversight independent labs have, and what the potential ramifications would be for this kind of human experimentation. I'm going to stop and say this right now: I Am Not A Scientist. I am just a very curious person who likes to read and do deep research about various topics, and have for my entire life. Any mistakes, assumptions, or inaccuracies should be taken with the "this is a work of fiction, exploring some concepts that could arise in the near future" label. Basically, my brain asked me the "what if" and then wouldn't shut up about it until I wrote this.

Like Tryst, I have been a radio DJ [as well as clubs and other places] and I tend to think in music/soundtracks for life. I trade tracks with people I care about and make them mixtapes, even though they're not on cassettes or even CDs anymore. The officially unofficial soundtrack I compiled for this book is available to stream on several services, and you can hear some of the tunes that Tryst and Fo trade with each other, as well as songs Tryst would stream on her radio show or listen to during the events of ASLID. You don't have to check it out; it won't hurt my feelings. But the music is a part of the story and the mood and lyrics reflect that. The links are always available on my website, christianeknight.com.

ACKNOWLEDGMENTS

As always, I have the best support system and they deserve a shout-out. First up is my editor, Fiona Robinson. Without her this story would read a lot more like some pages out of my journal, and not a fully-formed novel! I'm also lucky enough that she and I get along perfectly and share so many of the same interests, which makes working with her the best. You can find out more about her services at editingsmart.com and tell her I sent you.

My alpha readers, who get to see my work before anyone else including an editor does, also happen to be two of my most treasured people. My partner Christopher patiently sat on the edge of his seat as I dribbled the words to him in cliffhanger fashion, and knew when to cheer me on and when to ask probing questions for clarity. He's a visual artist but well read, often preferring literary work, so when he likes what I write it's a huge compliment. He makes me feel powerful as a writer, and so, so loved. Stacie Strickland, the best bestie and an excellent writer herself, read everything and immediately sent me several messages. [Which I screenshot and now live on my phone where I see them every day.] The parts that meant the most to me:

"I think that was my favorite thing that you've written so far."

[...With a big circle around the sentence "Let his optimism not lead him to disappointment."]

"I love this story so much! You'd better publish it!"

...Like I had any other choice, ha. Fo and Tryst needed to get out of my head and into the world. But seriously, Stacie is always there to lift me up when I'm feeling the consequences of choosing writing as a career. If I'm stuck, she helps talk me through the problem, and if I'm excited about a scene she cheers me on. She's my number one brainstormer partner and writing would be a lot more lonely without her, and so would my life.

I couldn't do any of this without my mom, Judy. I'd be writing but the probability that anyone would read it would be extremely low. She's been my backer, my cheerleader, my advocate. She's the one who saved my first story that I wrote when I was six, and will tell you all about it even now. Thank you Mom, I love you. Even if you deny that my weirdness came from your side of the family.

I'd be remiss if I didn't mention my hardcore group of supporters. They've believed in me since the beginning; thank you Connie Byrne, Melisa Morrison, Janica Carter, Professor Greenman, JaneA Kelley, Kirsten Westrate, Velma Root, Brandon Thomas, Kent Thurman, Megan Congdon, M Bickers, Kate White. Special mentions to Dianna Gunn and the Weeknight Writers community, Strong Women–Strange Worlds, Balticon & BSFS, and SFWA, all of whom have contributed to my growth as a writer and author and supported me in various ways. I wish I had room to mention everyone who I love and treasure, but please know that you mean the world to me and I would fight your [theoretical] weird brain scientist parents for your autonomy anytime.

Can't forget all the musical artists that gave me inspiration, were there to fill out the atmosphere, and built the soundtrack to my life, and to this book. A special mention to my beloved Bangtan, who will never see this but just in case: you really did save my life–and gave me a reason to start studying Korean. Thank you for the music, and for sharing a little bit of your hearts and souls with a million strangers.

Lastly, a huge shoutout to all the message boards, chat apps, and other online spaces where a lonely person craving deeper connections could move [mostly] anonymously and spill their innermost thoughts to other mostly anonymous seekers. Those spaces aren't as ubiquitous as they used to be, but I'd like to think that we'll find our way back as social media becomes less welcoming as it succumbs completely to late-stage capitalism. We need liminal spaces where we can explore connection in ways that give us freedom, rather than forcing us to perform or conform. We need the risk of sharing ourselves with strangers as a way of truly being seen.

That's what this story is, after all.

www.ingramcontent.com/pod-product-compliance
Lightning Source LLC
LaVergne TN
LVHW050957080826
845145LV00009B/2328